DEADLY DEPARTURES

DEADLY DEPARTURES

Ted Allbeury

This title first published in Great Britain 2007 by
SEVERN HOUSE PUBLISHERS LTD of
9–15 High Street, Sutton, Surrey SM1 1DF.
Originally published 1976 in Great Britain only
under the title *Italian Assets* and under the
pseudonym of *Richard Butler*.
This title first published in the USA 2008 by
SEVERN HOUSE PUBLISHERS INC of
595 Madison Avenue, New York, N.Y. 10022.

British Library Cataloguing in Publication Data

Allbeury, Ted
   Deadly departures
   1. Riviera (Italy) - Fiction
   2. Suspense fiction
   I. Title
   823.9'14[F]

ISBN-13: 978-0-7278-6576-2

Except where actual historical events and characters are being
described for the storyline of this novel, all situations in this
publication are fictitious and any resemblance to living persons
is purely coincidental.

All Severn House titles are printed on acid-free paper.

Typeset by Palimpsest Book Production Ltd.,
Grangemouth, Stirlingshire, Scotland.
Printed and bound in Great Britain by
MPG Books Ltd., Bodmin, Cornwall.

To my mother –
who will receive an expurgated copy

One

As I put the starboard engine into reverse the stern settled in alongside and I cut both engines. I got the stern rope round the bollard and threw the bow rope up to Mario. On the 'diga' alongside were Mario, the harbour-master, and a girl in a white bikini.

The harbour-master was there to collect his two bottles of Glenfiddich that kept me my berth at Santa Margherita. Mario was there just for Auld Lang Syne, and because he was my agent on that beautiful bit of Italy they call the Costa Ligure. And I guessed that the girl was there just to watch a boat tying up, and to torment the local talent. She was a real dish. Long blonde hair that was blowing in the hot noon-day wind, and one of those startlingly beautiful faces that are still going to be beautiful in fifty years' time. The big blue eyes were watching the operations with a faint amusement that kept the square white front teeth on show. She was about eighteen, tall and slim and big breasted, and she stood unconcerned with her long legs apart, as if she didn't know that the thin bikini briefs only emphasized the space between her legs.

1

I rigged up the gangway and Mario came down first, holding a fistful of mail and a couple of small packets. Signor Guardelli, the harbour-master, came down too, my mooring certificate in his hand. And that left only the girl. As I looked up at her she smiled, and as I looked down she bent down and held out an envelope.

'Mr Farne?'

'*Si Signorina.*'

She laughed. 'I'm English, Mr Farne. Signor Lunghi asked me to bring you this letter.'

As she leaned forward the magnificent breasts were breathtakingly on view and as I took the white envelope I managed to look up at her face. She was grinning, and the blue eyes were amused.

'How'd you like to come down for a drink?'

The long hair swished as she shook her head, still smiling. 'Maybe some other time.'

And she stood up and waved as she walked off along the quay. All the alongside boats were dressed overall as they say in the Navy – but with staring men, not flags.

Away from the bright sunlight, in the shade of the saloon, the boys were sitting at the teak table. I threw the envelope on the pile of mail from Mario and started my hostly duties.

From the harbour-master I got the news of two boats for sale and four prospective customers. And the bad news that the council were considering charging for fresh water for boats in the harbour. He took his two bottles of malt and departed as if he couldn't wait to get at it.

When he'd gone Mario put his legs up along the foam cushions and leaned back comfortably, looking at me.

'How long you staying, Max?'

'September, October if the weather holds good.'

'I've transferred about twenty-five thousand to your number two Swiss account.'

'Twenty-five thousand what?'

He smiled. 'Sterling. For the Cleopatra and the Fjord.'

'Who was the pretty bird?'

'Her name's Gabby. I don't know her family name.'

'And who is she?'

'She's one of Carlo Lunghi's seraglio.'

'Tell me more.'

Mario leaned back and sipped his whisky.

'Lunghi runs a night-club here in Santa Margherita and another in Camogli. And he fences 90 per cent of everything that's stolen south of Milano and as far east as Livorno.'

'I wonder what he wants with me?'

Mario nodded towards the pile of letters. 'Open it and see.'

It was an expensive envelope, stiff and thick, and on the back was dark-red sealing-wax, and the imprint of a dolphin or a seahorse. It wasn't too clear. I ripped open the envelope and slid out the letter. It was typed and signed with a big scrawl. The type was unusually large and the signature was in green ink.

> Villa Camogli
> Santa Margherita
> 12th May

Signor Farne,

I have some business to discuss with you. Contact me soonest.

> Carlo Lunghi

I shoved it across to Mario who flattened the sheet and read it carefully. He looked up with raised eyebrows. 'What d'you think?' I asked him.

Mario shrugged. 'Up to you, Max. I should go. It might make life easier while you're here.'

'In what way?'

He pushed the letter aside and sighed. 'He's got influence everywhere, and he's got some very rough boys.'

We gossiped for an hour and I fixed to have my evening meal with him and Mafalda. When he had gone I checked over the boat and listed the work that needed to be done. If you buy and sell boats you need to be a shining example to both buyers and sellers, and the trip from Chichester had left its marks. There was three days' work for me, and I'd have to get the Volvo man across from La Spezia to check the engines.

When I had washed and shaved I walked into the town, changed some travellers' cheques at the bank, bought some fresh food and some wine, and then strolled back to the boat. She was a 42 footer, a 'Sealion' made by Meakes at Marlow, and she was my place of business and my home.

I've got permanent moorings in Birdham Pool and continuous options on moorings in Santa Margherita, Piraeus and Tangier. And as I'm not resident anywhere I'm not a tax-payer either. Like the old lady who sent her tax-form back: 'I think it's a great idea but I've decided not to join.' And no lawns to mow and no mortgage to pay. The boat was paid for and there were two accounts in Zurich with enough noughts on the end to keep me happy for quite a time.

I showered and changed and took a bottle of chianti with me on to the afterdeck. Then I opened the mail and sat in the sun as I read. A letter from a girl in Hamburg and another from a girl in Paris. One would be heading my way in July and the other in September. A leaflet from Decca Navigation on the latest model radar, three cheques for final payments on boats I'd sold and delivered, and a sharp note from HM's Inland Revenue asking me to establish how many days I had been in the UK in the previous fiscal year. The smaller packet was a spare set of fuses from Sony for my CRF220, and the other packet was a flash-shoe for my Nikon. No bills, and no solicitors' letters.

The bay of Santa Margherita is the nearest thing I've got to a home. I like Italy and I like Italians. Although it was May the sun wasn't getting through the haze that sat on the side of the mountains. The sweep of the hotels was lost as it curved up to the Miramare barely visible as it jutted into the sea and the curling mist. You could just see the people on the beach, and there was a bus disgorging passengers in the square by the bank. The noise of the Vespas and Lambrettas carried faintly over the water, the modern Italian summer substitute for the buzzing of bees in clover.

About eight I checked the warps, rolled the gangway on to the sea-wall, and headed for Mario's. It seemed a long time since I had seen them both but, in fact, it was less than a year. We sat in the garden with scampi and salad, and the stars were out by the time we got to the coffee.

Mafalda put the tray with the coffee and glasses on the white garden table between us and left us alone.

When he was pouring the brandy, Mario said, 'How've you been, *amico*?'

'I've got by, Mario. Kept myself busy and all that.'

'Have you been to see Lunghi yet?'

'No. There's no hurry.'

He turned to face me. 'How about I phone him now, and I'll drop you at his place?'

'Oh to hell with that, Mario. I'll get a night's sleep first. Let him wait.'

And that was that.

I left just after midnight and as I walked down the hill from Mario's place I tried not to think of Tammy and Gianni. And that was probably why I didn't see the Fiat until I was almost on top of it. It was parked in deep shadow against the jetty wall and as I walked on, a man who was leaning against the car's bonnet straightened up and walked slowly towards me.

'*Buona sera, Signor.*'

'*Buona sera, cosa c'e?*'

'Signor Lunghi sends his compliments and asks if you come with me to see him.'

'Tell him I'll come tomorrow afternoon.'

And it was only then that I saw the knife. Maybe he only lifted it so that I should see it, but all that had got left over from the war-time training at Beaulieu was reflexes, and although he was strong he was too young and too inexperienced. I guess that usually when he flashed his knife, people did what they were told. And that's not good training. I could feel the strength in his arm as I forced down his hand towards me, and when I released the pressure, his wrist came forward and I pressed down on the back of his hand. And he screamed as the knife clattered on the cobbles; and as his sinews gave, the joints opened and then cracked.

Then I heard the car door and the others came for me in a rush. A pistol with a silencer hissed and flashed, but the bullet went whining out to sea. As I concentrated on the gun hand I only saw the pipe as it passed my face and thudded into my left shoulder, and then I blacked out as something hit the back of my head.

When I came to I was sitting in a big leather chair with carved arms and my left arm wouldn't move. My tongue touched two loose teeth and there was a very salty taste. There was blood down the front of my safari jacket. And there were four men sitting watching me. One was tall and young, and very handsome. He was wearing a cream suit and held a glass in his hand. He was looking at me and smiling as he half sat on a long table with one elegant leg swinging slowly as he sipped and watched. Welcome to Italy, wish you were here.

I guessed that the other three were the thugs from the car, and there was a splinted bandage round the big one's right wrist.

The tall man put down his drink and turned towards me.

'Well, Signor Farne. It seems that what I had heard about you is true.'

He waited for a response but I just stared back through my one good eye.

'I had the doctor check you over. He says that nothing is broken. Extensive bruising and you'll not feel too good for maybe a week. It was quite unnecessary, of course.'

'Too bloody true it was unnecessary, so why did they do it?'

'You misunderstood the situation, Signor. That's what caused the trouble.'

'Maybe the police won't agree.'

And when I saw his smile I knew then that he'd only said it to make me respond. He was swinging his leg again and his smile was forbearing and amiable.

'I've already mentioned the incident to the police.'

'And?'

'And they agreed that it was an unfortunate accident.'

I moved slightly and the redness came behind my eyes at the pain. He pointed to a bottle on the table beside my chair.

'The doctor left those for you. Says they'll ease any pain. It's up to you.'

'What is it you want?'

He nodded and stood up briskly. 'Of course.' He waved at the three men and they shuffled across to the door and left.

I looked around. It was a big room furnished with great taste, an unusually happy mixture of old Italian and modern Scandinavian. The carpets were thick and expensive looking and the paintings on the wall were skilfully lit. Lunghi dragged a heavy chair across the floor and sat down not quite facing me, as a gesture to my swollen left eye.

He offered me a cigarette from a gold case and there were jewels on the lighter as he leaned forward to light it for me. He leaned back and lit a cigarette for himself, and as he sat back he was relaxed and in command. He stretched his legs out, exhaled and turned towards me.

'We talk business? Yes?'

'You talk and I'll listen.'

He smiled faintly. 'I should like to buy your boat.'

'Which boat?'

'Your boat. The one at the jetty. She's called *My Joanna*, isn't she?'

I shook my head and it nearly blinded me.

'She's not for sale.'

'Say forty thousand?'

'Forty thousand what?'

'Pounds sterling.'

I screwed up my good eye to get a better look at him. 'You can get a new one for half that.'

He shrugged. 'Maybe. I want to please you.'

'Take me back to my boat. That'll please me.'

'Sure. I buy the boat and you take it back to England for me. You stay on board and I pay you to look after it.'

'What the hell is all this? What are you after?'

He smiled and reached for another cigarette.

'I told you. I want to please you.'

'Why?'

'I want you to help me. I want to consult with you.'

'For God's sake, Lunghi, you don't have to have me beaten up to get my advice. You just pay me the same as anyone else does. Boats are my business.'

He looked at me carefully. There was no smile now. I could see the big brown eyes looking me over while he worked something out. His tongue moved along his lower lip reflecting his anxiety or his doubts.

'The advice I want is not about boats.'

'What's it about then?'

He shook his head and stood up, and my head creaked up to see his face. He looked down at me, his face serious.

'I tell you when we have done our boat deal. I buy your boat cash. Forty thousand sterling. In ten days you take her back to England for me. I give you signed transfer form so you can have her back for free in one month's time.'

'But I'm staying here until at least September. If we do the deal she's yours and I should buy another boat to live on here in Santa Margherita.'

He pursed his mouth and his beautiful Italian-made shoe spread imaginary cigarette ash on the carpet.

'No, the deal would be like this. You take her back in a week or ten days. I have her for maybe two days' fun before you go. When you are back you buy another boat for you perhaps. This boat stays mine for one month.'

'You know that boats like mine are registered and if they're sold there are legal documents of transfer.'

His hands spread wide in Italian protest.

'OK. OK. We do it every way legal.'

'If I did this you would do it through Mario del Bruna?'

Again the protesting hands, the shrug, and the big brown eyes. 'But of course. No question.'

I looked at Lunghi. He was about thirty or thirty-five. Handsome, elegant, obviously rich, and clearly the best kind of wrong Italian.

'Give me one reason why I should do this, Lunghi.'

His mouth opened quickly to speak, and then it closed. He looked at me speculatively, weighing up some pros and cons. And then he said quietly, 'I will not say about money, or force, I just say that I ask you to do it because somebody once helped *you*.' He waited. Expecting a question. So I asked it. 'Who was it who helped me?'

'You remember a night last year, and you sat in a taxi near the Ponte Lumbro in Milano, and a white Lincoln convertible stopped and a man got out and spoke to you?'

'Yes. I remember.'

'I drove that car for Gianni Podoni.'

'Tell me more.'

'I was with him in his apartment when the waiter came with your message. I drove him to your taxi and back again to the via Torino. Then he sent me back here. I was one of his men. I looked after the south, along the coast to La Spezia. I was driving the car when they killed him. They thought I was dead!'

I remembered that night all too well, and the things that happened afterwards. And thinking made me sad again. Even Carlo Lunghi didn't look too happy, but that was his worry.

'OK, Lunghi. I'll do what you want. Within reason.'

He was all smiles and obvious relief, as if I'd solved the world's problems and he got the royalties for it. There was the pressing of bells, and the popping of champagne corks, and my last vision as I started to flake out was three pretty girls absolutely starkers. When I came to, there was a light down the end of a tunnel and the sound of a bird. As the light came nearer it became a window, and as I leaned up on my good arm the sound of the bird was the lovely Gabby talking to Lunghi, who was leaning against a dressing-table alongside the window. Gabby was sitting on my bed, no longer talking, but looking at me.

'You've had a long sleep,' she said. As if it mattered a lot.

'What time is it?'

'It's about ten o'clock. But you've been asleep for more than a day.'

I could hear my slurred voice and I wanted to sleep again. 'I didn't switch the lights off on the boat. The batteries'll be flat.'

I heard Lunghi say, 'I've had her checked. The lights will be OK. You didn't put them on.' And then the waves carried me down and under again.

The next time I was conscious I was standing at the side of the bed. They must have given me an injection and my feet were like lead. I couldn't move but I could see. Gabby was holding a book as she watched me. She reached across and pressed a bell and Lunghi came in almost immediately. He looked at me.

'The drug will soon wear off. D'you want to go back to the boat?'

I nodded because no words would come out.

An hour later I could move around slowly and I sat at the big table in the big room feeling like Mussolini signing the odd death warrant as I signed the buff transfer form transferring 64/64ths of the motor vessel *My Joanna* and her 'guns, ammunition and appurtenances' to Signor Carlo Teodoro Lunghi. Mario sat serious and po-faced as the ceremony proceeded. Lunghi signed a bank draft in my favour for billions of lire and I passed it over to Mario to transfer to Zurich.

Two

L unghi's white Jaguar decanted me alongside the boat and they took the hint when I waved them goodbye. Mario had stayed up at the villa to complete the transfer formalities.

There was a breeze coming in from the bay and the boat was shifting uneasily on her warps but the familiar movement under my feet was a reassurance.

I switched on the big Sony radio and tried the 25 metre band. There was a Glenn Miller recording from New York, and to the strains of 'Take the "A" Train', I looked over the boat that was no longer mine. Second-hand she would make seventeen thousand, but if I were buying her I shouldn't have gone past fifteen and a half. I'd need to look around for a new home.

It was cold enough to need some heating and I took a mains lead out to the plug on the jetty and switched over the transformer. It looked like it was cocktail time on the gin palaces riding their buoys just out from the sea-wall, and I wondered why Carlo Lunghi didn't buy one of those boats instead. And I wondered what the consultation was all about.

It was just getting dark when the gangway rattled, and as I angrily swung open the wheelhouse door Mario was feeling his way down with a bottle in each hand.

Inside the saloon he sank back against the cushions waving a hand at the bottles. 'For you Max, from your admirer Signor Lunghi.'

'What's the bastard want now?'

'Nothing. He really is an admirer.'

'You could have fooled me, my friend.'

'Is the boat OK for the journey back?'

'No. I'll need at least a week to prepare her, and I'll need the Volvo engineers from La Spezia.'

'I'll get Carlo to fix that.'

I sat down and reached for one of the bottles.

'What the hell is it all about, Mario? You got any ideas?'

He shook his head. 'No idea at all, Max. All I know is that he wants to talk to you on Sunday. I've no idea what it's about but he's concerned you should like him. And he wants to take this boat Friday and Saturday.'

'Where's he taking her?'

'I've no idea. I asked, and he didn't even acknowledge the question. He just asked me to influence you to co-operate with him.'

'OK. Influence me.'

Mario smiled half-heartedly and shrugged. Despite everything it was nice to be back in shrugging country again.

'His men were stupid. They're only used to gang fights. He tells them to bring you back. They bring you back.'

'*Was* he one of Gianni's men?'

'Sure he was. I wasn't one of Gianni's admirers, as

14

you know. He wasn't my kind of man. But Lunghi was probably rated as his second-in-command. One of them anyway.'

'Did Gianni trust him?'

Mario grinned. 'You know Gianni, Max, he didn't trust anyone. You were the only exception.'

'Any idea why he wants the boat to go back to England?'

'No ideas on anything, Max. No ideas, no clues.'

'Can you fix me a place for the two days he has the boat?'

'He says you are his guest at the villa.'

'Like hell I am.'

I pushed in the corkscrew and heaved out the cork and poured us a drink. When he'd taken a sip Mario said, 'Take my advice, Max. Just do as he asks. Don't make any more trouble.' He saw the anger and indignation on the half of my face that still moved and he shook his head. 'Drink the wine, for God's sake.'

I did, and it was fantastic. I looked at the label. It was Chateau Mouton Rothschild 1961. Lunghi had good taste in wine if nothing else. And as I thought it I realized that even that was unfair. He was as attractive in his blackguardly way as Gianni, and his villa reeked of good taste.

After Mario had left I sat at the saloon table and tried to sort out my thoughts. Mario had the money for the boat and Lunghi had the transfer deeds. It really *was* his boat now. I was literally homeless. A guest on Lunghi's boat. I contemplated doing a quiet bolt and catching a train to Genoa. But they'd take it out on

Mario and I should end up with no boat and no forty grand. If I headed out to sea they'd have a coastguard cutter alongside me in half an hour and a Ministry of Marine writ nailed to the saloon door five minutes later. Lunghi was still expecting me to advise him. What about, I had no idea, and I wasn't all that curious. I just wanted some peace and to ply my trade.

Still on the saloon table was my list of boat jobs and I read through it to find something not too strenuous to take my mind off the problems.

I stripped down the hand control on the searchlight and found the loose cable, and then I went up to the afterdeck and doused the davit mechanism with Plusgas. One of the locking pawls was seized up solid. It took less than ten minutes to free her but if you left those things, on a dark night in even a Force 5 when singlehanded it could mean that at the worst you didn't survive, and at best you were minus two fingers. The best tip I ever gave to clients was always to sail with efficient cowards. Boat heroes are generally dead heroes.

I looked down the harbour-master's list of potential boat clients. One was a Greek merchant who lived up the hill near the olive-oil plant and another was Avvocato Mantoni whom I had met from time to time. I cleaned up and walked through the square, over the bridge and up the winding road to the olive groves.

The Greek's villa was set in a cluster of pines and as I went through the gate a tall man in a white linen suit came towards me.

'Can I help you?'

'My name's Farne. I came to talk to Mr Synodinos.'

He smiled and held out his hand. 'Panayotis Synodinos.

Let's have a drink in the house. It's cooler.' A servant came with a tray of drinks and we sat facing each other across the low glass table.

'You speak Greek, Mr Farne?'

'French, German, Italian and English. Very little Greek I'm afraid.'

He nodded. 'Well let us speak in English. I'm looking for a boat and they said you were the best man to talk to.'

'Any idea what kind of boat you want?'

He leaned back, smiling. 'I'm afraid I'm the only Greek who doesn't know one end of a boat from another.'

'Is it for pleasure, to live on, long cruises or a day boat?'

He smiled broadly. 'I have my wife, a son and daughter. Ten years old and twelve years old. I have this dream of sailing from Santa Margherita to, say, the Piraeus. As I drive in, the crowds cheer and my family have great respect for their sailor-father. Does that help?'

'Yes. It helps a lot. Now when you say sail I presume you don't mean sail because I think you would be better under power.'

He shrugged. 'Whatever you say.'

'Any idea of how much you want to pay?'

He laughed. 'I have no idea what any kind of boat costs. Whatever I pay will surprise me one way or another. I am in your hands, but let us say that money is not the problem.'

'Well now, let's look at what you need. I suggest you have diesel not petrol. That means less speed generally but cheaper running costs, reliability and no fire danger. You need a double cabin and two single berths. You'd do better to have two heads and showers so that your children aren't too much under foot. You should have radar but I wouldn't want you to have an auto-pilot until you're experienced. Any idea what the dream boat looked like, Mr Synodinos?'

He nodded. 'She's brilliant white, long and elegant and covered with beautiful blondes.' He smiled. 'My dear wife is a brunette.'

'Well, the white is fine, the elegant is out because she'd have to be 50 foot before you got elegance, the blondes are easy, they gravitate naturally to boats. I've got in mind either a Grand Banks 36 footer or a 48 footer.'

'Can you supply me with either of those?'

'I can do the 48 footer right now but it could take six months to find a good 36. Apart from that there's a hell of a difference in price. The 36 I could get you for about thirty thousand.'

'And you think the big one might be too big for a beginner?'

'Not at all. She would be better. A big boat sits more solidly and responds nice and easy. No, I just feel it's a lot of money, and maybe you could be just as happy with the smaller version.'

'Where is the 48 footer?'

'She's lying at Portofino.'

He smiled and nodded. 'I'd like to see her. When would it be convenient?'

'Let me telephone you. I'll go over her and we'll do a short trip and I can go over the controls with you.'

And that was how we left it.

* * *

Mantoni lived over a cafe behind the Hotel Lido. I pressed the door-bell and a few minutes later he had opened the door. He wore an old dressing-gown and slippers, and he waved me in with his cigar.

Anybody who judged Avvocato Mantoni by the appearance of his home would be making a big mistake. The furniture was peasant, mainly cane and leather, and there were books and files heaped on chairs and tables. Mantoni himself was fat and clumsy and the big eyes looked heavy with sleep. But if you saw him in court, as I had seen him in Milan, you realized that the brain in that big bald head was extraordinary. The big fumbling hands always found the right paper, and the hooded eyes that never seemed to look at anyone noticed everything in court, from the judge's mouth to the cut on the prosecutor's chin. He understood instinctively the motivations of all kinds of people. Even presenting the defence he seemed to be neutral. Just relaying the facts and placing them before the court without emotion. He made no gestures, was never histrionic, and sometimes gave the impression that he was talking aloud to himself. But every word was the right word. His grasp of the law was staggering and he had refused a judgeship a dozen times. As he generally defended the bad boys he was very, very rich.

He was breathing heavily as he poured me a glass of wine, and his cane chair crackled and creaked as he settled back like an elephant having a mud-bath.

'I heard you were back,' he said. And he looked as if he disapproved. And without waiting for an answer he said, 'A bit soon, wasn't it?'

'Who knows, Signor Mantoni?'

He pursed his lips and looked at his glass.

'From what I hear you're already mixed up in more trouble.'

'What did you hear?'

His big sausage fingers moved around in the papers on the bamboo table and he picked one up and handed it to me without looking at it.

'Tell me about that.'

I read the newspaper cutting. It was an advertisement for a small boat that some fool had converted so that its centre of gravity must be higher than the cabin roof. I passed it back to him.

'Forget it.'

He nodded. 'Why? It's a good price.'

'It's hopeless. The original would be reasonable on a small lake. The conversion makes it top-heavy and uncontrollable. What is it you want?'

He shrugged, and the wine from his glass slopped on his big hand. 'Just a boat so that I could have a little trip to Portofino or Fruttuosa. Tell me what it should be.'

'The widow of Del Rossi, the jeweller, has got a small boat that she wants to sell. Made in England. A 23 foot Cleopatra. Single engine, two bunks. Just right for you.'

'Good condition?'

'I sold it to him new. You'll have to pay her about five thousand dollars US, and reckon to lay out another two hundred for inspection and repairs.'

'Would you do that for me?'

'I'll do the inspection. The yard at Camogli can do the repairs. I'll take her round for you.'

'How much your part?'

I stood up. 'I'll do it for nothing, Avvocato.'

He motioned with his hand for me to sit down again. 'Has Lunghi told you what he wants you to do?'

'No. He's bought my boat, that's all.'

He put his head on one side and closed his eyes. 'Yes, I heard that. I don't understand that at all.'

'What's the rest of the story?'

He shook his head slowly. 'You'll have to wait till he tells you himself, *amico*. I'm just a retired lawyer, happy with the peaceful life.' He swirled his wine round in his glass and watched it settle. 'I'll tell you this, Farne. Lunghi is a dangerous man. He admires you because of the things you did for Gianni Podoni. But make no mistake, if you cross him, old history won't help you. You'll end in the sea or in the morgue, and there's enough bad feeling still left from the things you were mixed up in last year so that nobody'll lift a finger to protect you. I gather that it was Lunghi's men who marked your face, and I can tell you right now that you'd be wasting your time going to the police. Either you or Gianni killed Timonetti and one of his men. As always it's convenient to the authorities to assume that Podoni was the killer because he's dead. But if you step out of line they could charge *you* with the killings and they could hold you for as long as they wanted.' He heaved himself up. 'Meanwhile, *if* you can find the time, buy that boat for me and fix it up.'

It was just gone seven when I crossed the square and as I turned into the Corso Marconi I realized I was being followed. One of Lunghi's bully boys was plodding along about fifty metres behind me. I stopped at the kiosk and bought cigarettes and the *Corriera della Sera*. By the time we got to the via Garibaldi he was happy that I was going back to the boat. I gave him a wave and he looked quickly behind him to see who I was waving to, and then when he got the message he slowed down, spat, and stood watching me until I turned left at the sea-wall.

There was a nice little breeze blowing and I slid back all the saloon windows. I looked over the four shelves of cassettes and made the big decision. Max Bruch's Violin Concerto and Mrs Mills with a bit of sing-along.

They'd delivered new gas cylinders and I heaved those down and put on the convertors. Calor gas and Camping Gaz try to do one another in the eye by having different threads on their connectors.

I put the diesels on, and let them thump away for a bit with the switch on, to charge the batteries, and that meant reaching down below deck to take off the covers to let the gases escape. The last job was to check the lines. Out across the bay there were a few small white clouds. I put on two springs just in case there was a wind in the night. There was the Italian Navy's training ship, the *Amerigo Vespucci*, anchored in the bay, and they'd sent the boys up to reef everything and I guessed they knew the weather in the Bay of Tigullio better than I did.

I radioed the harbour-master to get the Esso diesel tanker down to me and I took on 250 gallons. They backed off down the jetty flattening a couple of stray buckets in the process and after they'd gone I cut the engines. When I was groping around trying to get the battery caps on again my fingers touched a piece of insulating tape and I remembered suddenly why it was there. I slid my finger back down the battery and the matching tape was still in place. I peeled down both tapes and reached under the battery mounting and found it. Over a year ago I'd taped the pistol in a safe place as a piece of insurance. I shook the polythene bag free of surplus bilge-water and brought it up to the dim light just below the teak gratings. I looked around casually to check if anyone could see but there was nobody on the jetty. I laid the dirty package on the switch mountings and fetched an old shirt.

When I opened the package on the saloon table the gun was in good condition. Two round rust spots on the barrel but those were from condensation. The original grease was thin from heat and it came off easily. I laid the bits and pieces out on the *Corriera della Sera* and stuck another cassette on the machine. Nobody does better music than Puccini for cleaning and oiling guns by; I hummed along with *Madame Butterfly*. By the time that she and Pinkerton had got to the balcony I had reloaded the chamber and had got one up the spout just for Auld Lang Syne. When Pinkerton was launching into '*Viene la sera*' my work was done and I leaned back and listened. That Pinkerton really was a heel and he did no good for us sailors. But Puccini must have fancied him because he got all the best bits. By the time they had got to the love duet I was thinking about Tammy. She would have loved this stuff and she had probably never even heard it. I was imagining us in a box at La Scala when the boat rocked. I shoved the Luger under the table and swept up my Bowie knife from the bookshelf in one continuous movement and then flung back the two louvred doors at the aft companionway.

The girl stood there smiling, her fair hair haloed by a light from another boat. She wore a white dress and as I stared she was silent and still. It seemed a long time before I spoke.

'What d'you want?'

'I just came to see how you are.'

'I'm fine, thank you.'

The wide, soft mouth was faintly amused. 'D'you want me to go?'

I held back the doors. 'Of course not. Come on down.' She was so lovely that inside the saloon the lights seemed dull and she seemed almost shy as she stood there. Then I came to and waved her to a seat at the table.

'How about a drink?'

'I'd love a coke.'

'And a coke it shall be.'

Sitting opposite I watched her face as she bent her head to the straws. The eyebrows curved gently and the lids on her eyes were full and rounded and they disappeared as she looked up at my face. She was smiling. 'Are you really all right now?'

'More or less.'

She sat up straight and I tried not to look too long at the big round breasts. But when I caught her eye again it was obvious that she had noticed me looking. The smile was still amused. 'You look at me like Italian men look, but you're not Italian are you?'

'No. My father was a Scot and my mother was German. I was born in Paris, maybe that explains it. But maybe it's because I've been around Italy for a long time.'

'You were here during the war, weren't you?'

'Yes. That's when I first knew Gianni. Did you know him?'

Her head came up quickly and the soft mouth opened

to say something, then she thought better of it and she said, 'Carlo said that you were welcome to stay up at the villa if you would like.'

'No thanks.' I must have said it too quickly because she frowned and it made me want to smooth the furrows from the broad brow.

There are lots of pretty girls up there,' she said. 'You'd have a good time, you know.'

'I'm happy with the one down here. Can you stay for dinner?'

There was no coyness, no ritual. 'Sure I can, if you'd like me to.'

'Will Lunghi mind?'

She smiled. 'I'm not Carlo's girl, if that's what you're thinking. He's my guardian. My legal guardian. Anyway he sent me down to see you. He sort of likes you and he doesn't want you to be lonely.'

I looked across at her and I could see that she actually believed it.

'I'll take you for a meal in Rapallo.'

'Fine.'

I put on a Jacques Brel cassette and got out my shaving kit. I was scraping away and I leaned over to quieten the music.

'I suppose Gabby is Gabriella.'

'Yes.'

'And who chose Gabriella?'

'My father.'

'Was he English?'

There was a long pause and I turned round to look at her. The big blue eyes were wet and she was shaking her head. 'No, he was an Italian.'

'A lovely name,' I said, and I turned up the wick on Jacques Brel.

We had queued for the bus to Rapallo but we didn't make it. I took her hand and walked her across the piazza to where the little carriages were lined up under the palms along the promenade. We took the first *carrozza* and the driver flapped the reins to get up enough speed to take us up the hill out of the town. At the crest of the hill we could see the lights of Rapallo laced over the hills like dew shining in the sun on a spider's web. It was Saturday night and Rapallo was the nearest thing to the flesh-pots, east of Genoa. The sky was that ridiculous dark blue that is special to the Mediterranean and Drury Lane musicals, and everywhere was silent and still. She hadn't taken her hand away so I sang her a little song and the driver whistled the counter melody through his teeth ... *'Com' e bellezzioz' andar' sulla carrozzella, sulla carrozzella sott' il ochio del' mia bella.'* When it was over she gave us a clap and the driver turned round and said, 'You here in the war, *signor?'*

'Yes.'

'Prisoner of war?'

'No.'

He turned to take a good look. Then he pointed at me. 'You were the English with the partisans. You were Podoni's friend. They kill him, you know. Last year on the road to Brescia. He was a big crook. We like him plenty down here on the coast.'

The hand in mine held very tight and the lovely face was looking away from me towards the bay. He trotted us round to the Club di Roma and we got the big welcome from Giulio. And when we danced, the band managed to recall a few ditties from the '40s to please the old codger with the pretty young blonde. Every man in the place would have gladly cut my throat to take my place, but civilization prevailed. And Giulio had once been an all-in wrestler. The kind you're supposed to love to hate. And Gabby, in her white silk dress, lapped it all up and when I asked her if she went out much she shook her head.

'Carlo prefers that I stay at the villa. But sometimes I go out with him and Gaia.'

'Gaia, is that a tall girl, black hair and . . . very attractive.'

She laughed. 'You were going to say she has a big bust. Yes, that's Gaia.'

'Comes from Milan.'

'That's the one.'

The band were playing another English tribute with an every-man-for-himself arrangement of 'Tie a Yellow Ribbon' when I noticed a man watching us. What made me suspicious was that he was looking at me not Gabby. And Giulio was watching the man. The band changed over to a waltz and I like waltzes so I concentrated on what I was doing, because Gabby was tall enough for her cheek to be against mine as we danced and I hadn't done that sort of thing for a long time. By the time the music stopped and we had walked back to our table I had forgotten about the man and we were setting to on trout with almonds.

I was telling Gabby some silly joke when I noticed the silence. When I looked round the band weren't playing and like everyone else they were looking at Giulio and the man who had been watching me. The man had been wearing a bow-tie, blue with white spots, and it hung over Giulio's arm as his massive fist held the man's shirt in a bunch at his throat. And with his other hand he was slapping the man's face. The place was silent, and as we watched, the man sagged at the knees and Giulio passed him over to the door-man who shuffled him through the swing-doors to the kitchen. Giulio gave one of his masterful nods to the band and the place was nearly normal again. The big tenor was singing 'The highs are the highs of a woman in love' and waiters were getting about their business.

We were eating lemon sorbet when Giulio came across to the table. He bowed and scraped to Gabby and pulled across a chair from the next table and sat down. He spoke in Italian and his language was straight out of the Palermo gutters where he'd learned it. I pointed out quickly that the *signorina* spoke good Italian and he apologized profusely but with no great conviction. He put his hand on my arm. 'What I want to say, *amico*, is that that bastard wants to make trouble with you. I see him watching you long time. At first I thought he looking at the lady. OK we all have a look at the girls. But then he check your name with Federico and when he say you are Signor Farne he say he want to speak with you. He say he got message for you from Franceschi.'

'Who's Franceschi?'

'Never you mind, *amico*. You don' know him and you don' wanna know him. He is trouble and he not make trouble down here. Not in my place.'

He patted my hand, gave Gabby his polite smile while his eyes crawled over her boobs, and bowed off towards the kitchens.

Just after midnight they did us a last waltz and I sang her the words in French. Tino Rossi used to do it better but '*J'attendrai*' has taken a lot of punishment in its time.

We found the same driver, asleep in his carriage, and the thin horse with his head resting on the Campari sign at the edge of the pavement.

I put my jacket round Gabby's shoulders and we trundled back along the coast road. I had my feet up on the front seat and my arm round Gabby and we looked up at the stars. There was the beautiful smell of mimosa and peach blossom.

When the buggy stopped near the top of the hill I thought we might have to get out and walk the last hundred yards to the top, and when the driver didn't holler for our co-operation I sat up and looked around.

A man was holding the horse's head and another was pointing a gun at me. He was the man from the club and there was still dried blood around his nose and mouth. He waved his gun for me to get out. I shook my head. 'What is it you want?' I spoke in Italian. He didn't have the look of a linguist.

'They're waiting in the car.'

I looked around but I could see no lights and no car. 'Where is it?'

He pointed towards a dirt road up the side of the hill. 'What do they want?'

'I am to give you his compliments. Signor Franceschi. He just wants to speak to you.'

I took Gabby's hand. 'Come on, sweetie. We might as well see what he wants.'

We followed the man up through the olives, over an old stone bridge and then I saw the Citroen parked alongside a wind-break of yews. There was a man leaning across the bonnet with a submachine-gun and it followed us as we stumbled in the moonlight to the car. As we got there the door opened and a man got out. He was smoking a cigar and the glow showed a big, hard face, flat nose and small eyes and a Che Guevara moustache. His skin was very dark and when he spoke he chipped off the ends of his words as all Sicilians do. Some women could have found him attractive, but not being of their number, I found him singularly ugly. He took a last drag on the cigar and sent it sparking in an arc into the olive bushes. You could still smell it smoking in the crisp night air. I thought he had a gun in his hand, but I was wrong, it was a torch, and as he switched it on the beam stayed on my face and then moved over to Gabby's face. It lingered on her breasts and then went down her long legs, and then it was doused. While he had been examining us he said that he was Stefano Franceschi and he had sent one of his men to ask me to meet him. There had been an accident but now we all had the pleasure et cetera, et cetera.

When the light went out I could see his face again as my eyes adjusted to the moonlight.

'Why did you want to talk to me, Signor Franceschi?'

His tongue probed his big teeth as he sorted out the words, his eyes looking me over speculatively.

'I wanted to warn you, Signor Farne.'

'What about?'

'About "who" not "what". I want to warn you not to get mixed up with Carlo Lunghi.'

He waited for me to say something but I stayed silent while he searched his teeth.

'You understand?'

'I'm not mixed up with Signor Lunghi and if I were I should not be asking your advice. Did you want to say anything else before we go?'

The piggy eyes showed a touch of anger but otherwise his face showed no response. He leaned his right arm along the top of the car, relaxed and sure of himself.

'I tell you just one thing before you go. You join up with Lunghi and you'll end up dead meat. I guarantee you that.'

And then he grinned. 'When you want to earn real money you contact me, eh. Just ring the Centrale and say you want to speak to Stefano Franceschi. They will find me.'

He looked sideways at Gabby; then, still smiling, he looked back at me.

'That is all, Signor Farne. You can go now.'

He pushed forward the torch. 'Take this, you can give it to my man when you get to the road.'

And he watched us as we walked back to the rows of olives and to the path down to the road.

I paid off the driver with an extra two thousand lire at the piazza. We walked over to the promenade and as I took her hand I was working out what to say, when she said, 'Let's go back to the boat.'

With the lights on, the music playing, and the wine in our glasses we were back to normal. I twiddled the knob on the big Sony radio and we went round the world for some soft, sweet music: we found it on Hilversum. I was pouring more wine for her when she said softly, 'Are you married, Max?'

'No. Was once, but it was a long time ago.'

'What happened?'

'We got a divorce.'

'No. I mean what made it go wrong?'

'We got married at the beginning of the war. I went away on overseas service and when I got back she was shacked up with an American.'

'And you were in Italy during the war?'

'Yes. Part of the time.'

'And you acted for Gianni in a court case and that's why he liked you so much.'

'I think so. Is it time I took you back to the villa?'

She looked surprised. 'I thought you would want me to stay on the boat with you.'

I tried not to look surprised. 'Is that what Lunghi told you to do?'

'No. He just said I should come and see you and make sure that you're not lonely.'

'He's certainly trying hard to make me like him.'

She laughed and shook her head. 'No. He just thinks that maybe you want a girl.'

I looked at her across the table. 'And what do you think?'

She smiled. 'Yes, I think you want me.'

'What makes you think that?' My little convent sweetie had certainly fooled me. But if they speak softly and use words of two syllables I always take it for granted that they don't play. No matter how many times I'm proved wrong. But it's one of the nicest surprises I know.

'You look at me that way and I could tell when we were dancing.'

I'd thought she hadn't noticed. The innocence of old

age. But she was still smiling and it was a friendly, understanding sort of smile. 'You wash the glasses and I'll get undressed.'

I've never taken longer to wash a couple of glasses and as the water swirled away I wondered if this was Lunghi's way of getting me involved. She looked so young and innocent but she seemed to know a lot about men. But she wasn't a flirt, she didn't give out any 'come-on'. Just went round looking young and beautiful. And when she was quizzing me it was always about Gianni Podoni not Lunghi. I wondered what the set-up was at the villa up on the hill. But you can only take so long on two glasses and I switched out the saloon lights and walked through to the state room.

She was using my old military hairbrush to brush the long blonde hair and there were dimples at the base of her spine. She put down the brush and turned smiling to face me, her head slightly tilted so that a beautiful curve ran from her neck along her shoulder. Her eyes looked even bluer and the wide mouth seemed to smile in a special sort of way that would be hard to describe. The whole of her face had a special look as my eyes took in the big, firm breasts, the smooth, young belly and the golden fleece between her legs. And it was then I made my big mistake. My mind half understood the special smile and the look on her face and I asked the question you never should ask.

I said softly, 'Why are you doing this?'

She shrugged and the full breasts trembled but I saw the tear at the edge of the blue eyes. She swallowed and couldn't speak and a tear ran down her cheek. I took my bath-robe off the hook on the back of the door and draped it round her shoulders and led her to the double bunk. I held her hand and looked at her face.

'Tell me what it's all about. Lunghi told you to do this, didn't he?'

'No, he didn't, Max. I swear it. He wouldn't give me instructions about anything. He's very kind to me, in every way. Truly he is. I did it because Gianni always talked about you. He said you were his brother. More than a brother. And I felt a great feeling for you because of that.'

'Did you love Gianni? Is that it?'

She nodded. 'Yes.'

'And you still miss him?'

'Very much. All the time.'

'Were you Gianni's girl?'

She looked at me and the tears were falling fast.

'In a way. But I can't talk about it.'

'Of course not.'

I stood up and pulled back the quilt on the bunk.

'Now you just get in there, and I'll make you a cup of chocolate and tuck you up.'

She was asleep when I got back. The fair hair spread over the pillow and her hand held a wet handkerchief against her mouth. I left one light on and closed the door.

I must have been asleep for an hour when I heard the car coming down the jetty, then I saw the lights. I remembered the Luger and fished it up from under the table. I waited in the dark as the car stopped and I saw Carlo Lunghi jump out and come over to the boat. I reached up and switched on the lights and walked to the saloon door. Lunghi was pulling on a white shirt and tucking it into his denim trousers. As I slid back the door he said breathlessly, 'Are you OK? What they do to you? What's going on?'

'You'd better come in.'

One of his stooges was putting his big foot inside the saloon door and he just got it back before I could slam the door on it. He stood outside on the deck trying to find something to hold on to as the boat rocked.

Lunghi wiped sweat from his face and neck and looked at me expectantly.

'Tell me about those bastards. I only just got the news. The driver told the police and they couldn't contact me. I was at Portofino. I've come straight over. Did they rough you up, or the girl?'

I pushed him on to the bunk and poured him a whisky. 'Who's Franceschi?'

Lunghi shrugged. 'When Gianni was alive there were two lieutenants under him, I was one, Franceschi was the other. Most of the men came over to me but some went to him. He wants to take over everything. I offered to split the territory but he wouldn't have it. Wants to fight it out. OK, I fight back.'

'And he thinks I'm joining you.'

For the first time I saw that arrogant smile again and then he grinned. 'Maybe you will, Max, when we talk.'

'Carlo, you're a crook, Gianni Podoni was a crook, but Gianni and I fought in a war together. You weren't even born then and that's what makes the difference. I'm not a crook and I'm not going to join you or help you in any way. You understand Carlo. No way.'

He still smiled and when he drank the last of the

whisky he put down the glass. 'How about another one, Max?'

I poured him a treble and put the cork back in the bottle. I sat facing him and he looked at me without blinking. Then he said quietly, 'You like the girl, Max?'

'Yep. I think she's a sweetie.'

'Would you help her instead of me?'

'Maybe.'

'She needs help.'

'I know. But not the kind of help you or I can give.'

His eyebrows came up. 'What's that mean?'

'She's pining for Gianni Podoni. She loved him. She told me she's still in love with him.'

His glass was halfway to his mouth and he lowered it slowly to the table. 'My God. You don't understand, do you.'

'Understand what?'

'You don't know who she is.'

'What's it matter, she was Gianni's girl.'

He shook his head slowly and the brown hand reached across for mine. 'She's Gianni's daughter, *amico*, not his girlfriend. He brought her up when her mother walked out years ago. She was a baby. Three years old, maybe.'

Three

I'd fixed with Lunghi to see him at the villa the next evening. Gabby had slept until ten but I had to wake her then so that I could get on with my jobs. I sent a boy up with a note to Synodinos and fixed for us to go to Portofino at two.

I checked on the widow's boat and did a deal with her for Mantoni. I phoned the yard at Camogli after I'd checked the boat. There wasn't much for them to do but her hull needed a good scrub down.

Synodinos was early and we were in Portofino in good time to catch the tide. He stood with us on the quayside looking at her and I knew the signs. He was already in love with her. I rowed him and Gabby out to the Grand Banks and tied up the dinghy. The cruiser's decks were wet because they'd put two anchors on and she was lying out of line.

I left Gabby and the Greek to admire all the teak and chrome, and went down in the engine room. The last time I'd looked at her the bilges were filthy. Owners seldom bother to look, they've got automatic bilge pumps and that's that. But a bit of solid grunge and they're just sucking air, the dirty oily water builds up, and in the end you've got half a ton of water swooshing up and down below the sole boards. Rich men have made rich mechanics this way. The boat doesn't respond to the wheel so they have the steering gear renewed. Or they pay for it to be renewed. The mechanic takes a shufti down below and cleans the filter, switches on the pump and has a quiet drag for twenty minutes while the junk clears. He's pumping a hundred gallons of pollution into the drink and the swimmers get it a couple of hours later. A hundred quid for new parts that were never supplied and thirty quid for labour. The owner's delighted that the steering's OK again, and the mechanic tells the yard that he charged a tenner.

The bilges were still clean and I checked the engine connections and switched on. When the smoke showed they were warm, I started them and they responded after a couple of thumps.

I went over the controls with Synodinos and then hauled up both anchors as she idled. By the time I got back to the controls she was drifting beam-on towards roughly half a million pounds' worth of luxury cruiser with a French flag. Her crew stood at the ready with rope fenders, mops and boat-hooks. I gave the starboard engine 3,500 revs and then a burst on the port engine and we went away as if we were heading for the double-oxer at the Horse of the Year Show. The stern never came nearer than six feet to the big cruiser but a ton of Omo couldn't have made more foam than we did. And then we picked our way at 1,000 revs through the rest of the gin-palaces riding at anchor and we were on our own.

Synodinos couldn't wait to get his hands on the

controls and I gave him another half-hour of demonstration. There *must* be something about Greeks and boats because he lapped it all up in his quiet way and when I left him to it he did well. We cruised for an hour and went round the cape past San Giorgio. We stood off San Fruttuosa and I showed him the basics of using the charts for visual coastal navigation. And we practised dropping and weighing anchor a time or two.

I let him bring her into Santa Margherita and I didn't take over until we got among the really expensive hardware. He and Gabby put down the anchors and I put both engines in neutral so that Synodinos could switch them off.

We sat in the saloon and already he looked like the owner. He smiled across at Gabby.

'How do you like it?'

'She's beautiful.'

He nodded and looked at me. 'I'll have her, Mr Farne. You do whatever is necessary.' There was no haggling, no mention of money. I guessed he would be a client of mine for a long, long time.

'Would you like me to arrange a mooring here with the harbour-master?'

'Do we have to ask him?'

'Sure we do. We have to pay him too.'

He looked amazed. 'You have to pay to moor a boat on the open sea?'

I couldn't help smiling. 'It's not quite open sea, Mr Synodinos. That's a few miles out. Your mooring will cost you five hundred dollars a year and I recommend that you take it for at least five years. If you don't use it that long I can sell it for you at a profit.'

He wasn't impressed with this introduction to the ways of the sea but nothing was going to stop him.

'Which do you prefer, letter of credit, or cash?'

'Makes no difference, Mr Synodinos. Whichever you prefer.'

'I'll send you an irrevocable letter of credit this evening. You let me have the transfer documents when they are ready.'

Gabby and I walked up to Lunghi's place and as we went up the side road at the back of the Lido Hotel the small shops were still open. There was a hat in one of the windows. It was on a stand, in solitary splendour. It was a straw hat with a band of black ribbon, and at the side was a bright blue cornflower, a poppy, and a white marguerite daisy. There was no point in trying it on because it was obviously made for young Gabby. But that didn't stop her from trying it, and quietly admiring herself from all angles. It was only the mildest vanity and it was all I ever saw.

Lunghi was in a white suit, sitting on the flagged patio and talking on the telephone. He waved us to the flowery white seats at the table and hung up the receiver a few minutes later. He wasn't an Italian for nothing, and he had to see the hat from all sides while the lady blushed with pleasure. One of the things I like about Eyeties is that they say nice things about *all* women. Old ones, young ones, pretty ones and plain ones. Mothers and grandmothers get the treatment too. I don't care how phoney it is, that's how it should be.

We had eaten with Lunghi and Gaia in the big room, and then the girls had left us to it. We moved to the big armchairs and a bottle of Dimple Haig. Lunghi was putting down his glass, carefully watching his hand so that he wasn't looking at me.

'You done it with her yet, Max?'

'Gentlemen don't ask such questions.'

'OK.' He grinned, and waved his glass around. 'So have you done it?'

'No.'

He looked at me carefully and said, 'There's plenty of pretty girls here, *amico*. They all do it. You're welcome to any or all.' And he waved his hand again as he put down his drink. 'And the little girl doesn't have to know.'

I nodded but I kept silent. Then he leaned forward, his face turned up to look at me.

'I would like the boat tomorrow, Max, and the day after. You stay here. Gabby will be here too. She'll look after you. Is that OK with you?'

'It's your boat now, Carlo.'

'I know but I want you to be comfortable.'

'That'll be OK. What time d'you want her?'

'Ten tomorrow morning. I'll come down with the car and you drive it back up here. In fact you use it while I'm away.'

Lunghi looked round the room as if he were checking that we were alone. He looked at both doors and at the two panels of windows. They were all closed. He turned to face me and I knew that I was going to hear what it was all about.

'Can I take it, Max, that whatever happens you will not tell anyone else what I am telling you tonight?'

'Does it concern murder?'

He shook his head, but not with real conviction.

'I am pretty sure it does not. But I am not absolutely sure. It does not concern future murder, if that is what you mean.'

'Carry on then.'

'When Gianni was killed it was very sudden, very unexpected. We had never talked about what would happen if he died. It had never seemed necessary. It was not that the subject was taboo, it was just never thought about.

'Franceschi was his man for the west of Gianni's area. Roughly west of Milano and north of the Pavia river. Up to Aosta and Lago Maggiore. His area included Torino and alongside the mountains down to Savona. South of the Pavia and including the coast from Genoa to La Spezia was my area. Also I looked after the area east of Milano up to Brescia. Gianni didn't operate beyond Brescia.

'The night they killed Gianni I was driving the car. I was hit in the arm and when the car hit the side of the bridge I was knocked unconscious. When I came to I was in hospital. Gianni had died about an hour after he was brought in. By the time I was conscious it was early evening. They said I must stay in for three more days because of the loss of blood. I phoned one of my boys and I walked out just before midnight.

'When I got back to Milano I took over. But Franceschi had had twenty-four hours' start. Some of the boys had gone over to him. Twenty, twenty-two, something like that. Since then we have been fighting it out.'

He stopped, reached for his glass, took a sip and

looked at me, waiting for some response. But it meant nothing to me. When Gianni was alive it was different. Like the man who knew Doris Day before she became a virgin, I'd known Gianni before he was a crook, when he came over the mountains to me, to beg for more Sten guns to shoot Germans. I knew Gianni when it was patriotic for both of us to act like thugs. When they blew the whistle there were other things I could do, but not Gianni. Even without the war he'd probably have been a crook, pimping in Naples, in a real life Catch-22. But with the war he was a leader of men at nineteen, and by the time it was over his grimness had melted into style. To me, the crookedness was left-over war, and I never spent time analysing it. Gianni was Gianni, and that was that. In a way some of Gianni had obviously rubbed off on Carlo Lunghi, but it was a veneer, an adaptation. No matter what Lysenko said, genetics always won, short-term environment didn't produce mutants for Russian wheat or Italian men. I think Lunghi must have picked up my indifference. He went on, 'I had two meetings with Franceschi to try and make peace. We shared out Gianni's assets that we could control. We went fifty-fifty. I agreed to that despite the fact that 60 per cent of the organization had come over to me.

'But an important part of Gianni's fortune was not shared out. Franceschi thinks I have it, or that I know where it is, or that I have some way of finding it. He's obsessed about it. He talks and thinks about nothing else. I think he is unbalanced in his mind about it.'

His face looked defeated by his seriousness, and his dark eyes were watching my face for a reaction.

'You said you wanted my advice, Carlo.'

He looked down at his feet and then looked up at me again.

'That isn't really true. I need your help not your advice.'

I shook my head slowly and decisively.

'Not me Carlo, I'm not in the market.'

He sat silently, his teeth chewing his bottom lip in indecision, then he stood up and walked over to a desk in the far corner. When he came back he was holding a piece of paper. He folded it flat and looked at it for a long time. Then he stretched out his hand and offered the paper to me. It was a brief letter. Handwritten. It said in Italian,

> Torino
> 21 Maggio
>
> Lunghi,
>
> I give you to midnight 20th June to hand it over. Not one second more. If not, then we start with the girl.
>
> F.

I read it again and then slowly handed it back.

'Is the girl he means, Gaia or Gabby?'

'Gabby.'

'Why don't you send her to a safe place?'

He shrugged. 'That's impossible, I assure you. Every move I make he watches. I do the same to him. The same will apply to Gabby.'

'He can't watch every minute of every day.'

Lunghi stood up and walked across to the fireplace

and picked up the red phone from the small table. He spoke into it quietly.

'Franceschi, *dove?*'

There was no pause. He listened for a second or two and then put down the receiver and turned towards me.

'At this moment,' and he looked at the gold watch on his wrist, 'at this moment 23.52 he's with the Mayor of Savigliano. They're playing cards and Franceschi is winning.'

'Can I use your phone?'

He waved me to it and as I reached for the hand-piece I said, 'What's the mayor's name?'

'I've no idea. The exchange can find out from the exchange at Torino.'

And that's what they did, and I dialled the number in Savigliano. A woman answered and I gave her my name and asked for Franceschi. It seemed a long wait before he answered and his voice was cautious.

'Who is that?'

'I asked them to tell you, Franceschi. This is Farne. Max Farne. Will you tell me what you're doing at the mayor's house?'

There was a long pause. 'What the hell is all this, Farne? What's going on?'

'Nothing's going on, I just want a plain answer to a plain question.'

Again the long pause. Then, 'We're playing cards.'

'Are you winning or losing?'

'Oh, I'm not counting. Maybe about square.' And then he laughed. 'You checking on me, *signor*, for your friend Lunghi? He will know without your help.'

'Where is he? Where is Lunghi?'

His hand must have gone over the receiver because there was just that blank noise like distant surf and then I could hear voices and finally Franceschi's voice. 'Lunghi is at his villa and you are there too. Don't play games, little boy.' And he slammed down the phone.

I walked back to the armchair and sat down opposite Lunghi.

'Why do they choose Gabby?'

He shrugged and his hands were outspread.

'She is Gianni's daughter and I am her guardian. I have an absolute duty to protect her. Franceschi knows that I would do anything to protect her.'

I waited for a moment so that he was looking straight at me.

'So where is Gianni's fortune?'

For a moment he hesitated, then he stood up and walked over to the book-shelves. He carried a volume back with him and held it up as he sat down.

'*La Sancta Biblia*, Max. I swear on this that I don't know. Only Gianni knew. He didn't share his life with us.'

'How do you know there is a fortune?'

Again the widespread hands. 'There is no doubt, Max. There were many years of his operation. What we shared out was only the tip of the iceberg. And there are other, important people who have an interest in this.'

'Maybe it's in a bank somewhere.'

He shook his head. 'That would not be like Gianni. It's possible of course and I have done some investigating but the results were entirely negative.'

'So what is it?'

'Cash maybe, precious stones, precious metals. Could be anything.'

'And you've no idea what it is or where it is?'

'Absolutely none. I swear it.'

'And what are you going to do?'

'Will you help me? For the sake of Gianni's girl.'

'How could I help you?'

'The girl lived just outside Milano and Gianni was there most days. She knows all about the other half of his life. He really did love her. She may know where it all is, without knowing that she knows.'

'Have you asked her?'

'No.'

'Why not?'

'Until now it didn't concern me. Wherever it was, it was Gianni's. I make all the money I need to make. Always happy to make more. But that particular stuff I don't want.'

'What has the girl got? How does she pay her way?'

'I pay for her. I will always look after her and I'll give her a dowry when she marries. If I'm around, that is.'

'Why didn't she get part of the share-out when Gianni died?'

'*Mamma mia*, sixty-four people had a stake in that. She did get a share. About ten thousand in sterling.'

'Franceschi agreed to that?'

'No. It was part of my share. It was chicken-feed.' And he looked embarrassed at the revelation.

'You didn't finish telling me how you thought I could help.'

'Spend time with the girl. Talk to her about Gianni. See if you can get a clue where it is.'

'You're sure we can't smuggle her out? I could take her on the boat. We could go at night.'

'And where do you pick up fuel next? They would do it, Max. Franceschi would drop everything to keep his word. He has plenty of influence. Same as me. He doesn't have my pull down here but he can do much as he pleases and get away with it. Don't forget that nobody knows how big this prize is. There will be people from Roma, Milano, Palermo, everywhere, who will be very willing to invest time and money for a piece of this prize. We could be talking about several millions – dollars not lire.'

'And if you find it?'

'I shouldn't play games, Max. I would share it out. Including you, of course.'

There were a lot of loose ends and a lot of unanswered questions but I didn't have much choice. Franceschi had given Lunghi thirty days, and according to my arithmetic six of them were already gone.

'What help can you give me, Carlo?'

'That means you'll do it?' And the dark eyes looked almost black with concentration.

'I haven't got any choice, Carlo. You know that. So what help can you give?'

He stood up and stretched, not lazily, but like an athlete before a race. He stood, legs astride and hands on hips, his head nodding as he made each point.

'More than forty men. Money. Transport. Experts at driving cars, opening locks and safes, two pilots, three sharpshooters. Lawyers, police, soldiers, radio operators, dozens of girls, and me.'

It was half past two and I stood up unsteadily, stiff and cold.

'When d'you want the boat?'

'About ten thirty. Why not just stay here tonight and then stay on while I'm away.'

'No thanks. I'll come back here tomorrow but I'd like tonight on the boat.'

'I'll get the car.'

'I'm gonna walk.'

'I'll walk with you.'

As we walked down the via Pagana and on to the piazza the streets were empty. It was hot, but I felt cold and I was shivering from a mixture of tiredness and apprehension. I was lightheaded, aching with the need for sleep, but my mind grinding on like some crazy machine.

Lunghi walked right to the boat and waited until I had unlocked the saloon door and switched on the lights. As I went back to the door I could see the white teeth as he grinned.

'Did you see them?'

'The couple by the fish-market?'

'Anybody else?'

'The girl at the window at the end of the jetty, but she was yours.'

He laughed and waved as he turned and walked back along the sea-wall.

I set the alarm for 7.30 and stretched out on the bunk still dressed. I pulled the duvet over me and closed my eyes. I could hear stones rattling as Gianni and I scrambled up the mountain track. There was the chink of the swivel on a Sten-gun sling and below us two machine guns were firing 'hose-pipe' with one-in-four tracers and I was trying to make out what the German voices were shouting when I slid into a sleep that kept me listening and ducking for another hour. About 3.30 we found a baby-girl on the side of the mountain so I gave up and staggered across for a brandy. I hate drinking brandy except to ease pain, but there was pain enough in my heart and my head.

Four

T he alarm notwithstanding, it was 8.30 before I awoke, and despite the restless night my mind felt clear and a few things had sorted themselves out while I slept.

I should have to tell Gabby that I was looking for Gianni's assumed fortune. I couldn't possibly keep quizzing her about Gianni's life without upsetting her. I hadn't told her that Lunghi had told me that she was Gianni's daughter, and I certainly couldn't let her know that she would be the first victim of Franceschi's killers if things went wrong.

Lunghi arrived with Gabby just before 10.30. I showed him the controls but he obviously knew his way around boats. He was going off straight away and when the diesels had been thumping away for fifteen minutes Gabby and I went up on to the jetty and I took off the bow rope and threw it to Lunghi. The boat's head came slowly away from the jetty wall and I unlooped the stern rope and held it in a single loop round the bollard. When Lunghi signalled, I uncoiled the rope and threw it to the afterdeck.

51

My things went easily into the Citroen's boot and when we got to the promenade I turned left instead of heading for Lunghi's villa. We followed the narrow coast road to Portofino, and I ignored the black Fiat that travelled along behind us.

I parked the car and locked it carefully and we walked up the hill road to the small restaurant whose gardens gave a panoramic view over the whole of the gulf. Look east and you could see the sparkling, white-faced buildings of Santa Margherita, and way over to the west you could see a line of fishing boats coming into the small harbour of Camogli. There was a small bower of roses with a wooden bench and I walked Gabby over there after I'd ordered our coffee.

With one eye screwed up against the sunlight she turned her face to look at me.

'We were all spoken to by Carlo this morning. Everyone at the villa has to see that everything is as you want.'

'Sounds great.'

She grinned. 'Why did you come here instead of going to Carlo's place?'

'Because I want to talk to you where nobody else can hear.'

She was smiling as she said, 'Sounds great.' I took the point. It did sound graceless and a bit condescending.

'I've got a problem, sweetie, and I need your help.'

'Am I the problem?'

'No. Remember the other night on my boat? Well I thought you were Gianni's girlfriend. Lunghi has told me that Gianni was your father. I ought to have realized but I never knew Gianni had a daughter. I must have seemed very clumsy.'

She put her hand on mine. 'You were very kind, and that's what I needed.'

'You know about the rivalry between Lunghi and Franceschi?'

'Of course.'

'What did Gianni think of them both?'

She frowned. 'I think he had respect for them both. I would say he saw them as equal, but I think he preferred Carlo because he was more sophisticated. He said Franceschi was a hot man and Carlo a cold man. And he thought that cold men lived longer.'

'You know that Gianni's interests were shared out between the two sides after he was killed.'

'Nobody told me. I assumed that that would happen.'

'And they gave you a share.'

'Yes. I think it was about twenty-five thousand dollars. Carlo looks after it for me.'

'Lunghi gave you part of *his* share in fact.'

She looked surprised but she made no comment.

'Franceschi thinks that Lunghi knows where a lot more of Gianni's fortune is and he's putting great pressure on him to hand it over.'

She looked up quickly to check my face. '*Does* he know?'

'I don't think so. In fact I'm pretty sure he doesn't.'

She nodded. 'I don't think so either. Do you think there was more?'

'I would think so, honey. Almost certainly.'

'And he wants me to say if I know where it is. And

he's unlucky. My father never talked to me about money. If I did know I'm not sure that I would tell him.'

'I think he knows that. And that's why the pressure has been put on me. Would you help me find it? If it exists.'

She looked away from me. Out across the bay where the sun sparkled on the blue sea. Then without turning her head she said, 'Yes, I would.'

'Why?'

She turned her head and the big blue eyes were wet again. 'Because you're like my father. He talked so much about you. It didn't sound like a war, and killing Germans. Everything was funny. I think he liked a lot of money and power, but most of all he liked breaking the law. He liked beating authority.' She was smiling. 'I think my father was born to be what he was – a romantic crook.

'You were an army officer with the partisans. They didn't have status while they were at war nor afterwards. Gianni always said that after it was over every man claimed he was a partisan. He despised the politicians and the establishment because of what had happened to him. But if he had had some sort of real background he might have been like you. The war was almost a blessing for both of you. It saved you from having to go around in peacetime proving that you were men.' She sighed. 'That's part of why I would help you but not Carlo.'

'And the other part?'

She smiled. 'Because I would like to please you.'

And then the coffee came, and the eclairs, and the millefeuilles, and the peaches. When we had finally finished and cleaned ourselves up we sat in the sun and talked.

She only vaguely remembered her mother. An English girl, and I gathered that she came from a vaguely 'county' background. Very beautiful but too self-centred to tolerate the sort of life that Gianni followed. Erratic hours, a bad reputation, and despite the great wealth she was ostracized by her Italian equivalents. There were more and more open quarrels, with Gianni sitting grim-faced as the insults were flung at him along with the china.

And then one night there had been the sounds of raised voices and screaming, and the small girl had stood at her window watching her mother fling case after case into the big American car and drive off in a shower of gravel. She had never heard from, or seen, her mother since, and she still fretted because her mother had not come to her room to say goodbye. She had the feeling that Gianni and her mother were not married, but on her birth certificate her name was given as Gabriella Maria Podoni. I remembered that Maria was Gianni's mother's name. I'd seen it on a gravestone in the cemetery near the Porta Volta in Milan. She knew her mother's forename was Katharine and she thought her surname was Barrington; her mother had talked about a family farm in Kent.

From the time that her mother left, Gianni had spent most of his free time with the three-year-old girl, and she had travelled with him whenever it was possible. School had been a convent not far from the villa where they lived. For as long as she could remember there had been armed guards at the villa and in the grounds, and she was taken and fetched from school in a chauffeur-driven car with dark windows. None of Gianni's girls had ever been to the house, but she'd seen them at the via Torino apartment, and she had guessed their rôles.

And, she told me, she would be eighteen on 30 June. I hoped she was right.

She had no chip on her shoulder about being deserted by her mother and she had survived remarkably unneurotic from the violent death of her father. Her nature was loving, but her attitude to life would have been considered strange in any girl with a normal upbringing. She exuded a fatalism that seemed to combine the stability and gentleness of the convent school with an awareness and acceptance of the sexuality and beauty of her face and body. She had an obvious knowledge of men and sex that had been revealed that night on the boat, but it was strangely innocent, as if she were lending her body for sex as she might share a meal or lend a book.

That she was willing to help me was clear, but whether she could seemed doubtful.

The same black Fiat followed us back to the villa. They made no pretence of going on up the hill. It just turned and went down about fifty yards and parked. I guessed there would be several watchers spread around the villa itself, and Lunghi's men would be watching the watchers.

Gaia had arranged for a real English tea, and we sat around on the patio with our dainty cups and thin sliced toast and apricot jam.

Not quite a year ago Gaia had slept in the same bed

as me, and I put it like that to indicate that there was no sex. It was a few days after Tammy had been killed, and the night before Gianni was killed. He'd sent in Gaia to comfort me. And pretty Gaia had stood there smiling and naked as I sat on my bed, and she knew too much about men to think I would make love to her that night. So she'd tucked me up and slipped in beside me, and as I lay there shivering she told me a gentle Italian fairy story about a man who shot a nightingale, and she'd slid her arm round my shoulders and sung me a quiet song. I couldn't remember the words.

I looked across at her. She looked just as young and just as pretty, and for some reason I needed to establish her kindness to Gabby, and I said, 'D'you know the story of the man who shot the nightingale?'

And Gabby nodded and smiled. 'Yes, my father told it to me many times.'

'And it was Gaia who told it to me.'

Gabby smiled. 'Maybe it was Gaia who told it to Daddy.'

'I was very, very unhappy one night and she told me that story and she sang me a song to send me to sleep.'

Gaia half-smiled. 'A good memory, Max. What was the song?'

I laughed. 'I can't remember.' And I realized that I hadn't laughed for days.

Gaia smiled and sang the first few words again. *'Roma non far la stupida 'stasera . . .'* She looked at me. 'It was not a good night that night, Max.' And she turned to look at Gabby. 'I went in there naked, to let him make love to me, and all he did was hold my hand.'

Gabby looked at me but she didn't say anything.

Then she stood up. 'See you at dinner, Max.' And she walked back into the house.

Gaia raised her eyebrows. 'I think she's left us to talk about old times, *amico*. Or to make up for lost time.' She looked at me intently. 'She's in love with you, Max. I expect you know that.'

'No. I didn't know. Maybe you're mistaking affection for love.'

She shook her head. 'No. It's partly because of your likeness to Gianni, and partly because she's alone. She doesn't belong here. And partly, of course, because you're an attractive man.'

'Has she got any boyfriends?'

Gaia laughed and shook her head. 'Can you imagine what a boy would have to be to get past Gianni, and now he's dead his ghost gets in the way even more. Every man is compared with Gianni so they're losers every one.'

'Tell me about her mother.'

'Beautiful, and a real bitch. Gianni treated her like a queen and she drove him mad. Tried to cut him down to size and then drove him mad with jealousy. It was a mercy she left him. He sent her money but that was the end of the line for him. After that I never heard of her. He never spoke of her.'

'And how about you?'

She shrugged. 'When he died I just closed my door for two days and that was that. I survive OK – provided I have Nembutal at night.'

Five

Lunghi was away for two days and I had spent them lazily at the villa. Apart from the servants, there were several men there. I didn't see them together but I estimated that there were six or seven. Some were Lunghi's hoods but a couple were strangers.

I had been shown my room and had taken up my kit. There was a long corridor with a thick-piled carpet and a line of doors on each side. I had walked down to the end where it turned right, and there were more rooms. There were cinerarias and begonias in pots on the windowsills, and slim metal bars at the windows.

I tried the handle of one of the doors. It was a thick, solid, wood door, and it opened smoothly and silently. The room was dark but there were flickering coloured lights. They came from a screen on the far wall. And on the screen a pretty blonde and an even prettier brunette were competing for the attention of what looked like a sailor home from the sea. You could tell he was a sailor from the mass of tattoos, and there were some positive indications that he was just home from a long voyage without female company. The girls were clearly successful in their attention-getting, which must have been helped by the fact that they were naked and athletic. The cutting was bad, and it jerked from female charm displayed, to an all-in wrestling sequence of three writhing bodies that included two submissions and a couple of technical impossibilities.

There were three of us watching the screen but it took two or three minutes before we were all aware of one another and then there was an unpleasant Italian blasphemy from the bed, and creaking as the film flickered to a stop. A soft golden light filled the room. The girl on the bed looked like a younger version of Catherine Deneuve. Blonde, big sad eyes and a soft, wide mouth. She was beautiful. All over. And her companion was one of Lunghi's hoods. The one with the splint on his hand. Even from where I was standing I could see that he was well on the road to recovery.

Carlo Lunghi's instructions regarding hospitality for me must have been quite sweeping, because the thug reached for his trousers under the impression that it was my turn. The girl lay on the bed, as the lawyers say, without prejudice.

I closed the door behind me and went back to my room. Gaia was there giving instructions to one of the maids. When the young girl had gone I remarked on the disturbance I'd caused. She gave me one of her shrewd Sophia Loren looks.

'You've only got to say the word, Max. There's four girls here. They're all pretty.'

'I'm an old man, Gaia.'

She snorted. 'Men. I suppose you've got young Gabby on her back half the night.' I returned her stare and she plumped up two pillows and patted the bed-cover into place.

The next day I'd had breakfast in bed and a two-day-old copy of the *Daily Express*. It all seemed a long way away. While I was taking my bath I thought about Gabby's mother. She must know as much about Gianni's movements and habits as Gabby did. May even be more aware than Gabby of what was significant. I reckoned I'd better pay her a visit.

I played chess and Monopoly with Gaia and Gabby all afternoon. If I had children I'd ban games like Monopoly, they breed a meanness of spirit that distorts the character. The girls played like hungry tigers.

In the evening I took them to the Miramare and we ate a long meal and I took turns with them on the dance floor, and tried to give an air of Omar Sharif crossed with Rex Harrison.

Gabby came in to sleep with me after all the creaking and door-banging had subsided, and when the love-making was over she leaned up on one elbow and looked at my face.

'Tell me about where you live in England.'

'I live on the boat, sweetie.'

'Yes. I know. But where?'

'At Chichester. Birdham Pool.'

'Tell me about it. Is it a marina?'

'No. The pool is old-fashioned, and just boats. Little ones and big ones.'

'So why there?'

'It's peaceful, and beautiful, and when you come from London and you leave Midhurst it feels like coming home. Nothing bad happens around Chichester. Not for me anyway.'

'So it's a hiding place?'

I opened one eye and looked at the pretty face. 'A sanctuary maybe. Anyway, you're a clever girl to see it.'

She said quietly, 'I wish I had somewhere like that, Max.'

'Was there anywhere like that when you were little?'

She shook her head. 'No. Everything has always been like standing on the edge of the sea and you can feel the wet sand pulling away with the tide under your toes.'

I stroked the long blonde hair.

'We'll find you a sanctuary all of your own, sweetie.'

She lay with her head beside mine. 'I'll ask you there, Max,' and her voice was sleepy.

Mario came up to the villa the following day with all the documentation on the sale of *My Joanna*. Lunghi had done everything he had agreed to. The boat was now his but he'd signed undated documents that would transfer the boat back to my ownership without payment at any time I chose after one month. And the full price had been transferred to my number 2 Swiss account.

The Greek's boat had gone through without any snags so it was a record couple of weeks so far as finance was concerned. I told Mario that I was probably going to be away for a few days and asked him to keep an eye on Gabby. He looked at me with those big brown eyes.

'Are you coming back, Max?'

'I'll be back, Mario, don't worry.'

He nodded. 'Are they still pressuring you, *amico*?'

'Nothing I can't take.'

When Lunghi came back he seemed very pleased with himself, but when I asked him about the boat and his trip he was non-committal except about a few technicalities concerning the diesels. He'd had new locks fitted at the yard at Chiavari, and he gave me a set of keys.

'It's yours to use as you want, Max. But you're welcome to stay here at the villa.'

'I'm going to London for a couple of days, Carlo.'

His face was like brown stone, hard with disapproval and anger. He shook his head. 'That's not possible.'

'It is, Carlo. I want to talk to Gabby's mother.'

He still looked suspicious. 'Maybe. But the girl stays here.'

'That's OK. But her mother was the only adult who knew what Gianni was up to when he was at the villa.'

He stood up. 'When you want to go, eh?'

'I'll go tomorrow.'

'I'll arrange for tickets on Alitalia, there's a feeder flight in the mornings from Genoa to Milano. That OK?'

'Fine, Carlo. I'll sleep on the boat tonight.'

He pushed out a waving finger, still suspicious, but aware of the logic of what I proposed.

'No tricks, Signor Max, or I cannot protect the girl. You remember that.'

Gabby had come down to the boat about seven that evening with the tickets and a timetable. I took her out to dinner and Lunghi looked in at the restaurant just before we left. To show that the all-seeing eye was still on me. He walked back with us to the boat and I invited him in for a drink.

We sat around the saloon table and Lunghi gradually relaxed. He wrote out a list of oddments that he wanted me to buy for him in London. He particularly wanted a tie like my dark blue one with the parachutes on. I wondered what the Special Forces Club would feel about Italian hoodlums walking around in the club tie. I came to the conclusion that most of them would heartily approve.

We escorted him up the gangway to the jetty, and as he walked away towards the lights of the town he looked a lonely, pathetic figure. As I put my arm round Gabby she echoed my thoughts.

'He's a sad sort of man, really.'

'He's a first-class bastard, sweetie, and don't you forget it.'

He came at six the next morning, and we all drove to the airport at Cornigliano just outside Genoa. They stood up in the observation area, and I waved to them as I carried my grip across the tarmac.

The DC10 circled out over the bay and then turned due north to Milan. I transferred at Malpensa for a flight to London with only a half-hour delay. By the time we were airborne I longed to be back in Santa Margherita. I missed that young blonde, and I realized that I actually liked having someone to protect.

It was hot at Heathrow, and the sun was shining, but nobody was singing, and nobody was laughing. This was English sun.

Six

There were a lot of Barringtons in the telephone directory, mainly majors and captains. But there it was.

BARRINGTON, KATHARINE, MANTIS COTTAGE, HOE LANE, MARDEN 217.

It was just outside the centre of the village, on the road to Maidstone, and I parked the car alongside a derelict oast. The cottage was Kentish clap-board, long and low with dormer windows and old red tiles. The gardens were well kept and the white paint on the house itself was pristine.

I used the heavy brass horse-shoe knocker and waited. A phone was ringing inside and it had that special empty sound that means nobody's going to answer it. I walked slowly down the flagged path to the gate and as my hand touched it a car drew up sharply, sliding to a stop outside the gate. It was a red MGB, its canvas top down and the narrow back seat crammed with boxes full of groceries and vegetables. The woman who was driving wore a silk scarf round her neck. She fumbled with the keys and then stepped out. With her hand on the car door she looked across at me.

'Is that your car parked by the oast?'

'Yes.'

'It's rather silly to park it there. It's a very narrow road you know. Most inconvenient.'

The road was no less narrow where she had parked but she had one of those faces that showed that she reckoned she was something special. She was very good looking and I could see Gabby's eyes and the pert nose. But the mouth had lost its generosity and there were creases of determination at each corner. She was used to being looked at and male admiration got no medals from her. I defied the antagonism and smiled.

'I'm looking for Katharine Barrington. I think she lives here.'

She pointed at the largest of the cardboard boxes. 'I'm Katharine Barrington. Perhaps you could take that one. Be careful. It's heavy.'

At the door she'd put up her knee to balance a box and her handbag as she groped for the door-key.

Inside, the hall was quarry tiled and cool, and the furniture was old and good. Like the garden, the place was well looked after. As she waved me through to the kitchen to dump my load I felt as African bearers must feel, standing around waiting for fresh orders. She came back with a string bag and another cardboard box.

Then she stood with her hand on her hip, the key-ring encircling an elegant finger. The big blue eyes looked me over and I returned the compliment. I could see what Gianni had gone for. The very pretty face and the fine bones, the long show-girl's legs and the magnificent breasts. Despite the ice-queen bit she wore no bra and the tips of her breasts were visible through the tight, thin sweater. They weren't on show because she couldn't stand men looking at them; her arms were carefully arranged so that I got the full display. When I looked back at her face the fine eyebrows were raised, truly supercilious, and she said, 'Right, what can I do for *you*?'

'Is it Miss Barrington or Mrs Barrington?'

'Miss,' she said, but her eyes were wary, and I could see a pulse beating fast at her throat. She pointed over my shoulder. 'Let's go through to the sitting room.'

She waved me to a club-type armchair across the other side of the fireplace from where she had sat down. She sat on an embroidered chair that was not so low as mine and I guessed that she was well aware that it gave a wonderful view of her superb legs. The backs of her legs swept down and along and into the cave of her skirt like Ernust Haas's photograph of the San Francisco bridge, and from where I sat I could see the white briefs that clung to her rounded behind. Her elegant arms cantilevered to where her hands rested on her knees and they didn't hide an inch of the pointed breasts. It looked like she was taking out insurance on the next question. She looked at me over the round-ness of her shoulder.

'I don't think you told me your name.'

'No. It's Max Farne, and I wondered if you could help me.'

'How can I help you?' And she was doing her stuff. Her mouth was open and she moved her jaw slightly and I realized that even jaws can be sexy.

'I want to ask you about Gianni Podoni.'

I was ready for her to explode, to faint, or to throw me out, but except for the white on her knuckles she was unchanged. But her voice was quieter as she spoke. 'And who are you to enquire about him?'

'I was a friend of his during the war and I'm trying to help his daughter.'

'In what capacity?'

'Trying to straighten out Gianni's financial affairs.'

'I can't help you. And if I could I wouldn't.'

'It's not me you'd be helping, it's Gabby.'

'I told you I can't help you.'

'I'm quite sure you could.'

'In what way?'

'Just talking about certain aspects of his life when you were with him.'

'It was fifteen years ago, Mr Farne. I've tried hard to forget all about it – Italy, Gianni, Gabby – the lot. I don't want to know.'

'I've no intention of interfering in your life here in any way.'

'Were you the officer who defended him in court that time?'

'Yes. But I'm not a lawyer.'

'What are you, a detective or something?'

'I buy and sell boats. I spend time in Italy and I met Gianni again last year. I expect you heard that he was killed.'

She nodded. 'I only found out last week,' and her hands gripped on her knees. 'I'm not going to say I'm sorry, Mr Farne, because I'm not. I'm sure he deserved it.'

'He didn't actually. He saved my life.'

She half-smiled. 'And now you're obligated to help his daughter.'

'I'm glad to help her if I can.'

'Well, I can't I'm afraid.'

'Would you try?'

Her face had grown two spots of anger and she was trembling. 'Let's get this straight, Mr Farne. In my book Gianni Podoni was a gold-plated bastard. I hated his guts and I still do. I left him for bloody good reasons. The charm didn't work for me, the big smile didn't work for me. I was just a front, the cool, calm, English rose he kept at home. That's all he wanted me for . . . and to have me as a change from his tarts.' She was shouting and I held up my hand and she stopped, the blue eyes staring.

'I'm sure you had your reasons for leaving. I didn't expect to talk about that part of your life with him.'

She sighed a deep sigh and shivered openly. Her eyes closed for a moment, then opened.

'Ask me then, for God's sake, ask me.'

'How about I take you out to lunch?'

She looked at me hard and there was a catch in her voice when she replied. 'You're another Gianni Podoni. That's just what he would have said.'

'And what would you have said?'

'I'd have said yes.' And she burst into tears. I drove her down in her MG and we lunched at the Wife of Bath at Wye, and as we chatted I noticed that she fished a bit to find out what Gabby was like. 'She's very beautiful, gentle, and a bit lost, but she'll find her own way. I don't want to say more because I don't want to tell her much about you. But if either of you tell me you'd like to meet the other I'll do my best to arrange it.'

'Ask me what you wanted to ask about Gianni.'

'There's nothing specific. I'm just casting around in the dark, hoping I might find a clue.'

'What are you looking for?'

'Could be cash, gold, diamonds – who knows?'

'I can't see Gianni storing money away. He'd want to invest it or get interest on it. Gold or diamonds are more like it.'

'Was the villa new? Did Gianni have it built?'

She looked at me strangely and her hand went in a reflex to touch her hair. 'What made you ask that?'

'He might have had a vault or a safe built in somewhere. In the foundations maybe.'

'Somebody asked me that question last week.'

'Tell me.'

'Somebody phoned from London. An estate agent. He said he was selling the villa and asked if it was built for Gianni.'

'What did you say?'

'I said yes.'

'What estate agency was it?'

'I've no idea. I don't think the man said.'

'Anything you can remember? His voice, for instance?'

'Definitely not English. More like an American.'

'Italian American?'

'Yes, that could be it.'

And for the first time I had the feeling that I was heading for disaster. She put her hand on my arm and her face was concerned. 'Why is that so bad?'

'It means that there are more people in the hunt than I thought.'

And I told her about Franceschi and Lunghi, but not about the threat against Gabby. Despite the rather arrogant appearance, this woman hadn't ever got over Gianni Podoni and it was easy to see how a girl with her background must have been agonizingly insecure with him.

'How did you meet Gianni?'

'My father was an officer seconded to MilGov in Milan and I met him frequently at our house.'

'Were you ever married to him?'

'No. He talked of marriage but in the beginning I didn't care. I was head over heels in love with him. And later on I knew it wasn't possible. I really did hate him. I had no friends, people just saw me as a gangster's mistress. I tried to change Gianni. He had enough property and investments for us to have lived a normal life. But he wouldn't change. Maybe he couldn't change, I don't know. He bought me anything I wanted but he lived his life away from me. At first I was desperately unhappy, but gradually it was anger and jealousy, and that didn't bring him back, it drove him away. But you won't understand because you're very like him. He always said so.'

Her hand was still on my sleeve, and I asked her, 'Did he ever take you on trips? For a holiday or a weekend, say?'

She put her hand to her head and her eyes closed as she concentrated, and she spoke slowly as she tried to remember. 'The only time we went away together was just after Gabriella was born. Gianni was picking up a new car – a Maserati – from the works. Where is that now – a dreary sort of town . . .?' She looked at me for help.

'Modena?'

'That's it. That's the dump. Then he took us into the mountains to a cabin.'

'Very high?'

'Yes it was, there were lots of chestnut trees and then the road to La Spezia went up higher to a pass – the Passo del something or other.'

'Passo del Cerreto.'

'That's it. That's the place.'

'And the place where there were chestnuts, was that called Collagna?'

Her eyes were wide with surprise. 'You know it. But it's the tiniest place. Just a few houses and a shop.'

'Gianni operated in those mountains with the partisans during the war.'

'We were there for a week.'

'What did Gianni do in that time?'

'Played with the new toy. Chopped wood. Did repairs around the cabin. Nothing special.'

We left the restaurant and I drove slowly back to her cottage. She seemed different, slightly more relaxed, and she laughed at a couple of jokes. When we parked outside the cottage I asked if I could use her phone.

In the sitting room she brought over the handset and I said, 'I'll pay you for this. It's to Italy and it's business.' I asked the overseas operator for Lunghi's number at the villa. There was going to be twenty minutes' delay.

While I waited she showed me round the house. It was very her, and very Sanderson. The kitchen was modern, full of Westinghouse fridges and washers and split-level cookers. But it was too clean, too tidy, it smelled lonely. When the phone rang she left me alone and I heard the operator ask for Lunghi. Then he was speaking.

'*Carlo Lunghi, chi parla?*'

'It's me, Carlo, Max Farne.'

'Hello. You made any progress, *amico*?'

'What's the name of Gianni's villa near Milan?'

'Villa di Roma.'

'Have you ever been there?'

'Yes, many times.'

'Since he was killed?'

'Three, four times.'

'Have you checked it over?'

'In what way?'

'For safes, hiding places in the cellars or the foundations.'

'Good thinking. I take some people up there tomorrow. Anything else?'

'Yes. How's Gabby?'

'She spent yesterday with your Mario and his wife and today she went down to the boat.'

'With an escort?'

'Don't worry. Everywhere she goes there is someone. When you coming back?'

'Tomorrow.'

'I arrange for you to be met at Milan at the airport. You got a flight number?'

'Not yet.'

'Doesn't matter, I get them to phone me from Alitalia. Anything else?'

'Give my love to Gabby.'

'OK. *Ciao.*'

She had done her hair and changed her clothes. The white sweater was even tighter and the thin black skirt clung to her hips and thighs. She was leaning against the doorway, smoking a cigarette as she looked across at me.

'When are you going back?'

'Tomorrow morning.'

'Would you like to stay here tonight?'

There was a tension and I didn't want to relieve it crudely, but I wasn't sure I wanted to be part of it. So I smiled at her. 'That would be nice. But I must move my car. It's very badly parked.'

She laughed and turned away, and said over her shoulder, 'Put mine in the garage and yours can stand on the drive.'

I sat on a tall yellow stool in the kitchen as she prepared our meal and I knew that she was enjoying herself. She must have been like this when she was first with Gianni.

We talked about boats and the people who bought them and then the call came through from Alitalia. I was on the 10 a.m. flight from Heathrow. Check in at 9.

When I went back into the kitchen she was reaching up for a tin of something and I reached up and took down the tin. And by some mad reflex my hands were cupping her breasts and as my fingers kneaded the firm flesh she slowly lowered her arms and stood unresisting as my hands pulled up the tight sweater. Her mouth came up to mine as she turned towards me and my hands closed over the smooth mounds, and as her arms went round me she moved against me in obvious invitation. It was then that the telephone rang. I counted to twelve and then she released me and walked through to the sitting room.

I could hear her voice but I couldn't hear the words, and then I heard her heels clicking quickly on the parquet floor.

'It's for you,' she said. 'It's from Santa Margherita.'

It was Lunghi and his voice was clear despite the distance between us.

'Max. I sent a team to the villa. Gianni's villa. The fire brigade were there, and the police. The place had been blown to bits. The reports say that it happened early this morning.'

'Any signs that they found anything?'

'My men couldn't get near, my contact with the police is on leave. He won't be back until tomorrow night, then I'll know more.'

'My flight is Alitalia 179.'

'OK. We'll meet you.'

I hung up and went out to the MG. When it was in the garage I walked back up the road to my hire car. When I switched on the headlights I could see him out of the corner of my eye. He was standing in the shadow of the oast but the light had touched his white shirt front and the cuffs.

I parked the car and went in the house. The curtains were drawn and the fire was newly lit, and she had taken off the white sweater. When the black skirt was back to her hips she had lain back to let me look. And when finally our bodies met her mouth moved avidly on mine. She drove me next day to the airport, and either the crisp May morning air or the previous evening had made her look younger by years. When the first flight-call came up she put up her mouth to be kissed and then said, 'Will you keep in touch?'

'Sure I will. Don't forget to phone the car people.'

She nodded. 'I'd like a photo of Gabby if it were possible.'

I smiled at her. 'I'm sure it will be.'

I waved to her as I passed through the swing doors to the ramp.

When I landed at Milan there was a cable for me on the board.

> FARNE C/O ALITALIA FLIGHT 179
> INFORMED MAN MADE ENQUIRIES
> YOU LAST EVENING IN PUB STOP
> AMERICAN ACCENT DARK 30–35
> LOVE KATIE.

I went to the wash-place inside the customs area and burned the cable.

Carlo was waiting for me in the forecourt complete with car.

'Is it convenient to go out to the villa?'

'Sure. Let's go there now.'

When we were sitting at the second traffic lights I said, 'How many of your team speak English, Carlo?'

'Three speak it very well. Two you could understand but they're not fluent. Why do you ask?'

'Just curiosity.'

He'd got the same instinct for lies that I had and he was silent all the way to the villa.

There were two policemen guarding the rubble, a photographer or two, and half a dozen long-hairs who looked like local reporters. There was a man in plain-clothes who was collecting bits and pieces in plastic bags. There had been five or six separate explosions and the boys had known their job. The front wall had come down in one piece and covered the drive and part of the lawn. The rest of the building was rubble and it had been blown so that the ground floor was clear except for the remains of the ceilings. Over to the right was a big pile of furniture and carpets and there were still small trails and wisps of smoke coming from the rubble. The cellars had been blown open by individual charges and the solid concrete had cracked and sagged and stayed put. Lunghi and I went over it carefully and the explosives expert told us how it had been done. It was a mystery, he said, as to why it was done with this strange mixture of expertise and stupidity. But if you knew they were looking for something that might be hidden there was no mystery; but we left him unen-lightened.

On the inside of the front wall as it lay across the drive there were still curtains at the big window frames, and pictures still in place. I wondered which was the window that Gabby had looked out from when she watched her mother leaving. Despite the sun I felt cold. Gianni, his woman and his daughter, would all have different memories and feelings for this house, but whatever they were, this was the end of this piece of their dreams.

I wondered why Franceschi had taken the devious route through London to Katharine Barrington, to check on the building of the villa. It seemed out of character. Too sophisticated. The deeds must be registered some-where in the Milan administration and somebody must have sold the land and done the building. Maybe he wanted to make sure that his enquiries gave no clue to Lunghi. But again, if he thought Lunghi *needed* such information it meant that he already knew that Lunghi really didn't know where Gianni's loot was hidden.

On the way back to the airport, and on the light plane to Genoa, I worked out an elaborate escape plan to helicopter Gabby up and out from Santa Margherita. But all escape plans boiled down to needing at least fifteen minutes with Gabby unobserved, and that was never going to happen.

When we got to the villa a man was moving a meter on a metal rod inch by inch over the floor, the ceiling and the walls of the big main room. It seemed he had done the rest and could confirm that the villa was unbugged.

It seemed it was part of the daily ritual for every modern Fagin's home. Almost a status symbol.

Lunghi stood with his arms folded, impatiently waiting for the man to go. When he had carefully packed his kit he nodded to Carlo and went through the windows to the garden. Apparently he gave that the electronic once-over as well.

Lunghi sat at the big table and waved me to a chair. He wanted to know what I had found out from Gabby's mother.

I gave him a lot of detail but nothing that gave him

a lead to the forest house at Collagna, nor about the phoney estate agent. But I did mention the man who had followed me. I kept silent about the cable. He looked suspicious when I'd finished but it may have been no more than his normal suspicion. And I was happy for him to absorb the fact that part of the cost of my co-operation was my independence.

'Did she ask about Gabby?'

'She was very hostile to Gianni, but she asked what Gabby looked like. I think she was mildly interested.'

'She was a real bitch that one, Max. Very English. Cold as ice. No wonder Gianni screwed around.'

'Anything happened back here?'

He grinned. 'I've been attending to our normal business. A bit of export to India.'

'What the hell do you export there?'

'Gold, *amico*. It's all they want. They pay high prices.'

'How do they pay you? What's better than gold?'

He shrugged. 'That white powder, *amico*. For Marseilles and New York.'

And as he said it the penny dropped.

I walked back to the boat and the black Fiat went berserk trying to follow me as I walked through arcades and narrow back streets. But we all arrived at much the same time at the fish-market and they watched me walk down the jetty.

Gabby was there. Sitting on the state room roof, swinging those long brown legs and trying not to smile too much.

I jolted down the gang-plank and walked round the deck to her. The late sun made her face golden. She was wearing an apricot-coloured dress and a pair of white sandals. When I leaned forward to kiss her she put her arms round me and rested her head on my shoulder.

'I'm glad you're back.'

'I'm glad to be back. What's that?' And I pointed to a big paper bag that was lodged against the hand-rail of the coach-house roof.

'Two kilos of peaches.'

I perched up alongside her and reached for the bag. They were big, beautiful, Italian peaches, and if you've never eaten a real Italian peach you've never tasted a peach. As I bit into mine it tasted like the smell of roses. Big, old-fashioned roses that shine in summer gardens and scent the air just as the light is fading. We paddled in peach juice up to our elbows and spat the fat red pits over the hand-rails into the bay.

When we were finished I lifted her down, unlocked the wheelhouse door and we stepped down into the saloon. As I reached back for my canvas grip I said, 'Are you staying here tonight?'

She was sitting with her legs up on the foam cushions, looking at me.

'If you'll have me.'

I bit back the obvious crack and avoided the big blue eyes by opening all the venetian blinds.

'You're just what I need, sweetie, and we've got a few things to talk about.'

'Did you see my mother?'

'Yes, I did, and she asked a lot of questions about you.'

'What did you tell her?'

'Not much, because I wasn't sure what you would want.'

'Did she talk about Gianni?'

'She sure did.' And I sat down facing her across the teak table. 'She isn't a fan, but if it's any consolation, I'm quite sure she loved him.'

I reached out for her hand. 'Men like Gianni and me have our good points but by and large we don't make good husbands.'

She shrugged and pouted her doubts.

'Don't shrug, sweetie. They didn't have a chance, Gabby. Anybody could have told them that, right from the start. They probably did tell them but it would make no difference.' I patted her hand. 'All I'm saying is, don't let you and me take sides. They both made one another very unhappy, so let's leave it at that. If you'd like to meet her I think she'd be over on the next plane.'

Gabby shook her head and the long blonde hair bounced at her shoulders. 'No. I don't want to see her.'

'OK. That's fine. And that's why I didn't tell her much about you, and I shan't tell you much about her. Where shall we eat, here or in town?'

'Let me cook for you here.'

'OK. Let's take a trip to the shops.'

With the spaghetti finished and the coffee getting cold we sat back and listened to Max Bruch's fiddle concerto and as a lollipop at the end, his sad, gentle arrangement of Kol Nidrei. When it was finished she asked what it was and I told her.

'What's it mean?'

'It's a sort of Jewish lament or hymn.'

'Jews and Italians are very like one another, aren't they?'

'Tell me.'

'Oh, they're musical, humorous, they cry all over the place. Big on families and children, but underneath it they're very tough. A bit like you and Gianni.'

'Did Gianni have any American friends?'

She screwed up her eyes. 'I don't think so. Not friends. But I can remember some Americans, two or three, coming to Milan. Gianni said they were businessmen. They came to tea and I can remember they sat in the garden talking.'

'What about Carlo, does he know any Americans?'

'Not that I know of. One came to the villa here for two nights but he'd been in jail in Genoa and he came to the villa while he was waiting for instructions.'

'What was he?'

'A crook of some sort.'

'Why come to Carlo's place?'

She turned her head and smiled. 'Don't you know? Can't you guess even?'

'No.'

'When any of the men have been in jail and they come out they come to the villa and Carlo gives them a holiday and let's them sleep with the girls.' She grinned. 'All part of the service.'

'Did Gianni ever talk to you about his will or how you would get by when he died?'

'No. He didn't believe in wills, and I'm sure he never thought about dying. He behaved like he was immortal.'

'Have you ever heard of a place called Collagna?'

'No, where is it?'

'Are you sleepy?'

She smiled with her head on one side, and she said softly, 'Will you take me to bed again tonight?'

When I'd checked the ropes and locked the saloon I went down the companionway into the state room. There was a double berth and a single berth, and across the beam there was a dressing-table and mirrors, and milady was standing there combing her hair and the dimples at the base of her spine were still there.

As I watched her she turned to face me and she stood with her long legs apart and her arms at her sides as I looked. There were shadowy pools where her shoulders converged beneath her slender neck, and her full, young breasts thrust out their heavy promise. There was a trace of muscle each side of the flat, firm belly, which swept down to the fan of blonde hair between her legs. She stood patiently as I looked, and then as I held out my hand she walked over smiling to the double bunk.

There were thoughts that I had to push aside as my hands enjoyed the firm breasts and the excitement between her legs, but they were lost in my eagerness to have her. And I took comfort from the love in her arms as she held me tight while her body eagerly accepted my lust. It was an hour before I had room in my mind for my guilt. It was her hand that woke me from my deep sleep and as I responded she pulled me to her and there was no more guilt, not even when the sun came up before we slept again.

Seven

I was up early the next morning and with a cup of steaming coffee beside me on the table I checked the route to Collagna and tried to fit some of the bits of the jigsaw together. But there weren't enough pieces to make even a corner, and I was conscious of the lack of progress and the short time that was left.

I went up on deck and looked towards the town. The sun made the long line of shops and hotels look like a band of shining white and the villas that spread up the hills behind stood out against the early summer greens and browns. Already there were figures on the beach and the sea looked heavy and flat.

There was a telephone kiosk at the side of the fish-market and I walked there slowly because the air was already quivering with heat. I checked on the phone that Avvocato Mantoni's boat had been serviced and brought back. It had been serviced and it would be back this afternoon, so I walked along to the square and then up the road behind the hotel. The cafe was already open and the tables arranged and I pressed Mantoni's bell.

He was dressed in a faded blue shirt and a towel, and he didn't speak, just nodded and held the door so that I could walk upstairs. He creaked down into the wicker armchair and waved me to a chair at the table.

'Pour yourself a drink. What's the position with my boat?'

'She's checked out OK, and they're bringing her back this afternoon. Mario can do the paperwork for you.'

He leaned back, his arms along the curved arms of the chair.

'I don't suppose you came along to tell me that.' The half-closed eyes watched me carefully and the thick fingers of his right hand were tapping against the chair.

'I'd like some advice, Avvocato.'

'Legal or otherwise?'

'Otherwise.'

He nodded. 'I'm listening.'

'You gave me a warning the other day, Avvocato. I'd like to know how much you know.'

He smiled frostily and leaned back as if he were blown by a strong wind. Then he chuckled and wiped his mouth with the back of his hand.

'I love that approach, Signor Farne. In the courts we call it "fishing", but not even the youngest advocate would be quite so sweeping as you.' He struggled to sit upright and looked at me with those fishy, wet eyes as he leaned forward. 'I'll give you the same warning again, Farne. Don't get mixed up with Lunghi. He's a successful, ruthless crook and nobody comes out of deals with him with their shirt on.'

'I didn't want to be mixed up with him. I had no choice.'

He pulled a face of distaste and swished his big arm as if he were cutting down thistles.

'*Mamma mia*, they all say that, Farne. All the petty thieves who get caught. Remember after we became co-belligerents what they used to say to you, '*Mai stato Fascisto io.*' The little pickpockets and the ponces I can forgive. They don't know any better. They say what they are told to say. You and Podoni are tougher men than Lunghi will ever be. So how is it you have no choice?'

'You know about the feud between him and Franceschi?'

He shrugged and pursed his mouth in dismissal. 'So thieves fall out. It's part of their life. They enjoy the drama, the self-importance. How does it affect you?'

'You know what the feud is about?'

His hands flew up. 'I can guess. Territory, who controls what.'

'I'm afraid it's more than that.'

His big head went back and his mouth was open as he looked at me. And his voice had changed. It was softer. 'Tell me.'

'They both want Gianni's fortune. The part that wasn't open and public like the buildings and the companies.'

He nodded slowly. 'Wasn't that shared out when he died?'

'No.'

'And because of your relationship with Podoni they think you might be able to help.'

'Exactly.'

'And why don't you just go back to London? You've sold them your boat.'

'First of all I'd never make it, and secondly there's another pressure.'

87

'What?'

I told him about Franceschi's threat against Gabby.

He wiped his mouth again with his hand and leaned back in the chair with his head resting on a cushion as he looked at the ceiling. Then without looking at me he said very quietly, 'They would do it, I'm afraid. We must think about this.'

He sat with his eyes still closed, his hand under his massive jaw as he rested his elbow on the arm of the chair. 'Any idea why Lunghi wanted to buy your boat?'

'He gave me more than it was worth. Maybe it was a disguised bribe.'

He shook his head. 'Lunghi would take it for granted that you would see that, and he wouldn't beat about the bush. If you refused a bribe he'd just raise it until you accepted. No, it must be something else.'

He sat silent for almost five minutes and then he opened his eyes and looked across at me.

'I think it would be wise of you to contact Franceschi. Tell him that Lunghi is willing to share the alleged fortune and that you have no knowledge of where it is, neither has Lunghi.'

'Do you think he will believe me?'

'Probably not, but he may concede some time.'

'D'you know him?'

'Yes. I've defended him once or twice as I have most of these men. He's another Lunghi. Older and rather set in his ways. Violence and threats are his usual weapons. He lacks Lunghi's brains but he's got a lot of protection. He must have because he's had his fingers burned a time or two but he's always survived. Lunghi himself isn't violent, he uses violence. Franceschi is as violent himself as his men. Rather old-fashioned. A brigand as much as a crook. You know how to contact him?'

'Yes.'

'See me again, if you want to, after you've met him again.'

I had no idea where Franceschi was when the Centrale connected me to him, but it obviously was not far away. What was more significant was that Mantoni had already spoken to him and had suggested that the meeting took place at the advocate's flat. I said I would see them both in an hour and I went back to the boat to tell Gabby I should be away until the afternoon.

Mantoni was dressed this time. In a clean white shirt and a black suit. Only his old slippers betrayed his real indifference to his audience.

Franceschi must have been there for some time for the chianti bottle was already half empty and there were cigar butts in the ashtray. Seen in full light Franceschi looked slightly less formidable. They were the usual brown Italian eyes but they looked at me as if he was impressed by what he had been told. His jacket bulged away from his massive chest, and I could see the grubby strip, that was part of the harness of a shoulder-holster. One leg was crossed over the other as he lounged back in Mantoni's wicker chair and he was using a toothpick in that ghastly cupped-hand fashion that some Italians consider the height of elegance.

Mantoni sat opposite me at the table and nodded to me to get cracking. I looked directly at Franceschi.

'Signor Franceschi, I thought it could save a lot of trouble if I spoke with you.'

He nodded and turned his head to one side to spit out a sliver of toothpick. And with this Royal Assent I went on.

'Signor Lunghi has told me of your interest and of your threat to kill Gabriella Podoni. Let me say that I have no doubt that Signor Lunghi has no idea where Gianni Podoni's fortune is hidden. He has asked me to help him find it, if it exists. For the sake of Signorina Podoni I have agreed.'

I stopped and waited for some response, but he looked without interest at his fingernails.

'Signor Lunghi is quite prepared to share whatever is found with you.'

And at that he responded. 'There is no question of sharing, *signor*. It will be handed over by the date I say or the action will be taken. And . . .' he said, wagging a thick, hairy hand at me, '. . . that will only be the start.'

Mantoni was watching me and I poured myself some wine.

'You realize that you are threatening a British subject.'

Franceschi laughed. 'I have made no threat against *you, signor.*'

'I don't mean me, Franceschi. I mean Gabriella Podoni.'

His eyes were alert. 'She is Italian. Her father was Italian.'

'Her mother is British and she was never married to the father. The child has the mother's nationality.'

Mantoni was sitting out of Franceschi's line of sight and he was shaking his head at me.

Franceschi's face was flushed and his voice was trembling with anger. He stood up as he was speaking and leaned with one hand on the table as the other crashed down again and again to set the glasses jumping.

'This is not a court of law, Mr Farne. And we are no longer ruled by Military Government. I make my laws in these parts.' He could hardly speak for his mounting anger, and his face was contorted. 'You go back to Lunghi and tell him it hasn't worked. Podoni's girl will be the first to go if that stuff is not handed over on that day or before. Lunghi's days will be over.'

He stared into my eyes and we were like schoolboys seeing who blinks first, or bad-tempered dogs circling slowly before they spring. I heard Mantoni's voice cut between us.

'Sit down, Franceschi. He's not the kind to be frightened.'

Franceschi sat down and then moved back in his chair.

Mantoni turned to face Franceschi. 'Would you accept me, Franceschi, as an arbiter in this?'

Franceschi looked at the elderly advocate and then stood up. 'No, Avvocato. There will be no arbiter. There are no choices.' He nodded to me. 'You tell Lunghi that too.'

He walked across to the door and let himself out without looking back. Mantoni sat looking towards the window, his fat fingers laced together. He was silent for a long time and then he turned towards me.

'Did you notice anything?'

'Yes. Franceschi was sweating across his top lip. He's scared of something.'

Mantoni smiled. 'I suppose we all notice different things. Fighting men look for signs of fear. Men like me look for other things.' He leaned back and made himself comfortable. 'You know, when I was in court I always used to feel that I should help them to talk. When a man opens his mouth he lets you look into his mind. Franceschi must have done anything at one time to be in my good books but this time he didn't give an inch.' He took a drink of his wine and carefully put back the glass. 'You know, I think there are strange pressures here. Franceschi didn't even hesitate for a second before he refused. He reacted like a frightened animal, a rat in a corner. I would have expected him to put up a pretence of considering a proposition if only to impress me with his reasonableness. But he didn't. Maybe *he* has no choice. Have you thought of that?'

'It's possible.' I stood up. 'Thank you, Avvocato, for your help and for your hospitality. I'll get on my way.'

He looked at me strangely, opened his mouth to speak, and then changed his mind. I was at the door when he said, 'I think you have more problems than you know, Mr Farne. I think you must consider your own position in this. Are you really so much obligated to this girl? What would Lunghi have done if you had not been here, for instance?'

I walked back to the boat slowly, and as I walked in the hot sun I tried to work it all out. There was Lunghi buying my boat. Franceschi's threats and his manic anger. There was the phone call to Gabby's mother, and the man in the shadow of the oast at Marden. There was the bombing at the villa, and right in the centre was young Gabby and the ghost of Gianni Podoni. I needed a few more clues, and although I didn't know it they were already heading my way.

Eight

There was a man sitting with Gabby in the saloon. He was about my age but slim and elegant and he had one of those fine, aristocratic faces that spell Rome in Fellini films. He stood up when I went in, and the bushy grey hair flattened against the roof before he bent to avoid the light strip. His suit was a medium blue and the cloth was surely Dormeuil, the cut Via Veneto. His shirt was silk and the blue tie had some circular motif that was hidden by the line of the lapel. His shoes were black brogues and the leather was unmarked.

He smiled as he stooped, and his teeth had been capped at film-star rates. He held out his hand. 'Monfalcone, Signor Farne. I do hope you will forgive my intrusion.'

I was tired of visitors, and letters, and watchers, and hoodlums, and I guess I didn't look too amiable.

'Could I beg a few minutes of your time?'

'What's it about?'

He smiled. 'Oh ships, and shoes, and sealing-wax, et cetera, et cetera.' And his accent was more Oxford than mine.

'What precisely?'

He looked round to where Gabby was sitting, pretending an interest in Reed's *Nautical Almanac*. Then the smile was back. 'Perhaps we could take a turn along the jetty?' We could have been rehearsing Jane Austen for a special charity performance at Bournemouth. I slid back the saloon door and waved him up the steps as I said to Gabby, 'I'll be five minutes, honey.'

She winked back at me and I wondered what he'd been talking about while he waited. Taking the waters at Tunbridge Wells, probably.

There were people he knew on two of the bigger boats and he waved back as they greeted him. And the handsome face was more royal than merely aristocratic.

At the end of the sea-wall he stopped, and we stood facing one another.

'I do regret the disturbance, Signor Farne. But my colleagues and I felt that I should contact you.' He waited for the ball to be patted back but I wasn't in the mood for social niceties. His mouth, I noticed, was compressed, the kind of mouth you saw in close-up on TV. They generally belonged to captains of industry or trade union leaders.

'I know you have some problems here in Santa Margherita and we think perhaps we could help you.'

'Who are *we, signor*?'

'Ah. I'll come to that later. But first let me ask you a direct question.'

He paused. The breeze was blowing his hair across his eyes and as his hand came up to push it back I saw a ring on his third finger. It was gold, with a circular top and a sea-horse deeply engraved in the circle. I'd seen the same pattern on sealing-wax a few days before. He watched my face as he started to speak.

'What did you learn from your talk with Miss Barrington?'

On the sea-wall behind him someone had painted in white 'Saint Clare helps Jesus'. And my God, at that moment I wished that she'd help me.

I'd had enough of the pressures, and people trying out their strength on me. My mind was clogged with details and conjectures, half-guesses and dead-ends. I needed time off from the treasure hunt. All my instincts were to face north and keep on walking. But it wouldn't do, so I launched myself into the ritual.

'Signor Monfalcone. I don't know who you are, who you represent, and it's none of my business. And what I learned from Miss Barrington is none of your business.'

'Signor Farne. I do most strongly recommend that you respond. The young girl, you yourself, and many others, are in great danger. It is pointless for you and me to play games. I think that you already know that. My people have great respect for you. There is no need for you to prove to me that you are not to be bullied. We know that. That is why I came to see you myself. Let me just say that we have a direct and legitimate interest in what you are seeking, and there is a question of discipline involved that is important. I make no threats beyond saying that the forces involved are beyond the defiance of any one man, or group of men. I have been brought from New York because of these problems and I must return very shortly. I ask only your help, your co-operation.'

95

He watched my face as I absorbed the glad tidings, and I watched him as I spoke.

'Are you Cosa Nostra?'

'There is no such thing, Signor Farne. It is a figment of journalists' and film writers' minds. I am a businessman.'

'What is your connection with Franceschi and Lunghi?'

'My colleagues have business connections with them both.'

'Who are you backing right now?'

'I don't understand.'

'Franceschi has threatened to kill Gabriella Podoni, Lunghi has used that to recruit me. Which approach do you approve?'

'These men operate the way they see fit, and they are two different types. And Lunghi has a formal responsibility as the girl's guardian that restrains him – so far.'

'And what would have happened if I had not chanced to be in Santa Margherita?'

'There's no point in hypothetical speculation, Signor Farne. You *are* here. The girl is the only person alive who might know where Podoni concealed this material.'

'She doesn't know, I assure you.'

'I accept your assurance. But she is still the only person alive who might provide the clues. She may know things without recognizing their significance. And you are the only person who could talk with her, and recognize as clues some casual recollection of something said or done by Podoni.'

'And why do you think I should have to accept this situation?'

'First because of the relationship that you had with Podoni. Secondly because of your affection for the girl herself, and finally because you must know that you would share her fate.'

'My life hasn't been threatened so far.'

He nodded. 'They probably assumed that you would take that for granted.'

The whole thing seemed a fantasy. Standing in beautiful spring sunshine, the smell of the sea and the noise of people on the beach, while a handsome man, elegantly dressed, gave me the good news that the result of not doing what they wanted was that a pretty girl and I would be killed. Not in bloody anger, but coldly, and no doubt efficiently.

'Signor Monfalcone, I think you should tell your colleagues that once you've threatened to murder two people there's no more pressure you can apply to them. I'm tired of you and your hoodlums jumping out of the bushes every five minutes. From now on take it that if you try any more pressure I shall raise hell with every official from the British Ambassador to the *guestura*.'

He looked at me hard as if to judge whether I was bluffing, and it angered me enough to underline my own threat. 'Don't think I'm bluffing, Monfalcone. Keep your hoods away from me.'

Those cold eyes looked at me for a second or two and then he turned and walked away. I watched him go and when he was about fifty yards away he stopped, turned round, then hesitated and turned back and continued towards the promenade. There was a big

Lincoln Continental parked there, and he flung himself inside. It pulled out from the sidewalk and went off in the direction of Rapallo.

There comes a time when the doctor tells you the bad news, so when I got back to the boat I sat down with a coke and told her the facts of life. There was no good pussy-footing around any longer. When I'd done my piece she didn't look all that worried and I asked her why.

'Well *you* don't seem worried.'

'True, but I've spent a life-time looking after myself.'

'What are you going to do now?'

'Your mother told me they spent a week at a place in the mountains just after you were born. I think we'll have a look at that and if we find nothing there we'll go up to Milan. Gianni was a Milanese by nature and I think that's where he'd salt things away. We'll see.'

'You think the Mafia control Lunghi *and* Franceschi?'

'No doubt about that. What did Slippery Sam talk about while he was waiting?'

'About New York and general chit-chat.'

'Put your sandals on. We're going on a shopping expedition.'

I bought solid shoes for both of us. Sweaters and jackets and denims for Gabby. And I hired a car.

I went back for the car about eight and drove her down to the boat. When our kit was loaded I locked up the boat, checked all the ropes and switched off the electrics at the batteries.

Twenty minutes later we were on the Autostrada

Azzure and as we went into the first tunnel I saw the black Fiat behind us. There were four cars between us when we left the last tunnel just before Sestri. By the time we were up in the hills of Borghetto they were back on our tail, and they were still there as we swept down to La Spezia.

The harbour was full as we drove up the Viale Italia and the lights flooded the square at the Piazza Italia. There were parking slots in front of the hotel, and as we unloaded I saw the black Fiat circling round the Piazza. They'd got problems. I wondered how many of them there were. They wouldn't know whether to book in at the hotel or to keep watch from the car.

We had dinner in our room and were early in bed. It was just getting light when we went down to the car the next morning and there was no sign of the black Fiat, but as we took the road to Aulla there was a red Lancia a hundred metres behind us. It wobbled a bit as I took the right fork when we left Aulla and I guessed they'd be doing some fancy map-reading. The wobble was because they took it for granted that I was taking the main fast road up to Parma. The road I had taken had a back route to Parma but it was itself the direct route to Reggio nell'Emilia. This was well outside Gianni's territory but we had both moved around it in partisan days.

The road was steep in places and we were already at the 2,000 feet level and going higher. It came down at Fivizzanno and then it was a long slog ever upwards to 4,000 feet, and the forests of chestnuts that were bright green in the morning sun. A mass of pink and white candles and a perfume that filled the car. I stopped about 20 kilometres outside Collagna and pulled into the side of the road. We sat on the mountainside with a thermos of coffee. The red Lancia had swept round the spur of the mountain too late to stop and they slammed on the brakes as they saw us. The car's tail wagged as the tyres slipped on the dew-wet road and they stopped a hundred metres further on. Nobody got out and they were too far away to be recognized. The registration was a Genoa number.

We sat there for half an hour and the thick turf steamed in the strong morning sun. I waved to the three men in the Lancia as we slid past them and their impassive faces stared at us coldly.

When we pulled up at Collagna there were more little shops than I remembered, and at the garage I asked if they could tell me the way to Gianni Podoni's house. They showed me the way on my map and warned me that the road up the mountain was rough and unmade. We had to reverse and go back the way we had come and the Lancia driver thought we were trying a get-away. He locked his car round viciously so that the front wing scraped the side of the bridge.

When we turned right at the little grotto with its pale blue Madonna it was almost a hair-pin bend, and the tarmac soon gave way to rough stones and pot-holes. The road, if you could call it that, was barely wide enough to take the car but it ran straight along the side of the mountain. Over to our right you could see for miles across the valley to the steep face of another ridge. In the valley itself were half-a-dozen small towns and immediately below a handful of small houses clung to the steep slopes.

'What are those mountains, Max?'

'They're called the Garfagnana. They're the spine along the Apennines.'

'How far to the cottage?'

I pointed ahead of us.

'I guess this is it.'

It was a typical mountain cottage. Pine and oak and a big circle in front to turn the car. And a double carport at the side. The air was cold at that height and there was steam rising from beneath the car's bonnet. There was an overgrown lawn in front of the house and beyond was a meadow with sheep.

I looked down the track and the red Lancia was groaning its way up the slope. I went back to the car and reached into the top of my hold-all and took out the Luger. I pulled up the slide and felt the round drive home. I told Gabby to lie down in the long grass in front of the house. She looked white-faced, but she did as she was told.

I leaned across the bonnet of the car and rested my arm till the pistol lay easy. The Lancia was about 150 yards away when I squeezed the trigger and for a moment I thought I'd missed. And then the windscreen went white, and birds flew up from the ferns and bushes on the side of the mountain. This team had taken over from the black Fiat team in La Spezia, and I guessed they'd done it in a hurry. The other boys were probably in the hotel while these watched my car. They'd have been told to tail me and I reckoned that they wouldn't have been given instructions about what to do if there was any resistance. I was sure they wouldn't come for us without specific orders. There was no point.

We were the only hope if they wanted Podoni's loot. Later on they might do something, but not now.

I kept the Luger lined up on the car and waited. They'd switched off the engine and in the mountain silence I could hear cow-bells down in the valley and the cooing of doves in the trees behind the house. It should have been the cue for Delius, but instead there was the noise of breaking glass as a gloved hand punched a black hole in the shattered windscreen. The wipers hung like spiders' legs and the gloved hand tore them from their bearings. Then the engine started and the Lancia slowly jerked its way back down the steep, rutted track.

Gabby was leaning up on her elbows looking through the tall grass and as the car disappeared she stood up and brushed down her jeans.

I jemmied the lock gently on the front door and it sprang back easily and the door swung open. There was one big room and facing us was a massive fireplace and a shaft of sunlight was on the half-burned logs in a pile of wood ash. There was a pile of logs alongside the fireplace. In the far corner was a low wooden bed with a wolfskin cover that was half on the floor. There were two old-fashioned chests and an elegant writing desk. Two paraffin lamps swung gently from the ceiling. The floor was red-tiled and over everything was a fine layer of dust. In the near corner was an old stone sink and a small bottled-gas burner, and the dark wooden door of the cupboard over the sink hung open, displaying blue china and some pots and pans.

It took us an hour's hard work to make the place shipshape, and the cedar wood that lined the walls smelled of pencils and schoolrooms as the soft breeze moved the curtains at the open windows. From the windows at the back you could see across the meadow until it fell to the dead ground of the mountainside.

While Gabby cooked the spaghetti I went over the big room. When you don't know what you're looking for it's all too easy to wander all over the place on the off-chance of finding something in some obvious place. I started with the far wall and went over everything inch by inch. After lunch I started again. I checked the car-port and a lean-to toilet while it was still broad daylight, and I did a quick check of the overgrown flower beds round the house.

I did a random check of the floor and took up a dozen tiles but there was nothing. I cleaned away the fireplace and stood up with a torch behind the stone chimney-breast. There was a mason's mark on the massive lintel but that was all.

There were two ancient pikes over the fireplace and half a dozen pictures on the walls. I took a couple down and checked the walls behind them. They were solid as rock.

When the sun was casting long shadows across the meadow I sat on the bed and eased off my shoes. I put another round in the magazine of the Luger and an extra one up the spout in case anyone was counting when we got down to gun stuff. I was looking across at Gabby as she turned away from the small stove and I saw her eyes go big and her mouth opened as she screamed. And as I followed her eyes I saw the man at the window.

Nine

He was about thirty and he wore the uniform of the *carabinieri* and as I headed for the door he knocked. He checked my face against the description they must have given him.

'Signor Farne?'

'Yes.'

'I'm sorry I frightened the girl. Could I have a word with you?'

I opened the door and went out to join him. He lit a cigarette and we walked towards the car. There was a bicycle leaning against the rear bumper. He leaned against the side of the car and looked sideways at me as he exhaled.

'Have you any authority to be up here?'

'The house belonged to Gianni Podoni. The girl is his daughter. It belongs to her now.'

He nodded. 'Are you staying long?'

'A week. Maybe ten days.'

'And the gun. Have you a licence to carry firearms?'

'A British licence, yes. And I'm skipper of a boat and entitled to a personal weapon.'

'There's been a complaint that you tried to kill a man today. You shot at him.'

'A car followed us from La Spezia and I thought they were going to attack us. I fired a warning shot in self-defence.'

He smiled rather frostily. 'Do you always shoot when in doubt, Signor Farne?'

'Nearly always.'

'The complaint was semi-official.'

'What does that mean?'

'It means I reported it to the mayor and not to the *questura*.'

'So?'

He smiled. 'So the mayor is Signor del Rossi and he sends you his warm regards.'

'Mario del Rossi?'

He nodded. 'I understand he was with you and Podoni during the war.'

'He certainly was.'

'And he recommends that you take my advice, Signor Farne.'

'And what's that?'

He dropped his cigarette and ground it out with his boot and then looked up at me. He spoke very quietly. 'My advice is that you leave very soon. Not longer than tomorrow.'

I smiled amiably. 'I'll take your advice.'

He wasn't smiling, he looked grim.

'There are people assembling in the village who are strangers but nevertheless well known. They certainly mean trouble. For you.'

And he walked to his cycle and waved as he walked

down the path. He hadn't been deceived by my bluff for a moment. No matter what I had said he would have accepted it. Mario del Rossi would have seen to that for old times' sake. But the warning was for real.

Our evening meal was not the most cheerful I've ever eaten, but I knew what we had to do. We were in bed before it was really dark and I told her about the times that her father and I had moved round the spurs and valleys of these mountains while the German patrols fanned out below us. When I saw her smiling, I stopped. She put her hand up and stroked my face.

'You don't need to do it, Max.'

'Do what?'

'Give me confidence. I'm as safe with you as I ever will be.'

And in case I mistook the point she slid back the silver-grey wolfskin and lay back as I looked at the lovely breasts so that their pink tips crinkled to inviting points.

I woke just after midnight, and almost without thinking I got out of the bed and walked over to the fireplace. There was still a dull glow from the logs we had burned, and I stood in their warmth and looked at the mantelpiece. There were some elusive dream-like thoughts in my mind, drifting like seaweed in a slow tide. And it was like knowing that you had dreamed but with no memory of the dream. It was something to do with being a little boy again. And breakfast. And a box with a picture on it, and another. And then it came seeping back with a catch-phrase attached. 'High o'er the fence leaps Sunny Jim. Force is the food that raises him.' And there was the pack of breakfast food with the man jumping with a packet of Force under his arm, and on that pack was a picture of it all again and so on until it got too small to recognize. And over the mantelpiece were the two ancient pikes diagonally crossed over each other, and there it was.

There was a picture, water-colour and Indian ink. It was a picture showing a door off-centre to the right. It was closed, but sunshine shone through the elegant fanlights. There was a tall window with inside wooden shutters that were held back to the wall with red silk tassels. And between the right-hand shutter and the door-frame hung a picture, the same size as the one that I was looking at. In the same golden frame with plaster roses at each corner. I'd seen that picture still in place on the wall of Gianni's villa as it lay across the gravel path and the lawns outside Milan, when I'd gone to see the destruction with Lunghi.

And I could remember the picture on that wall. It was of crossed pikes over a mantelpiece and a picture beneath them. The picture I was looking at now. I reached up to the picture to lift it off its hook. But the picture wasn't held on a hook. It wouldn't move. And as I looked closely I saw the gilt-headed screws that were in the centre of the roses at each corner.

I unlocked the door and walked to the car. There was a bright moon, and the mountainside was covered with a milky swirl of mist. The air was crisp and cold and I shivered as I opened the door. There was a set of simple tools in a fitted tray under the glove shelf. I lifted out the small screwdriver and slid back the tray.

The screws came out easily and I turned over the picture. There was a white cardboard mount with no

markings and four tiny brass sprigs that held the cardboard in the frame. I eased them out and lifted away
the cardboard backing. Inside was thin film with black
marks that looked like some cuneiform lettering of the
Middle East. I lifted out the film, replaced the cardboard and screwed the picture back on to the wall.

I lit the small brass lamp beside the bed and held up
the thin film. It was 10" x 8" but the film itself was
much thinner than normal photographic film, and much
more flexible. I folded it carefully and then opened it.
It didn't crease, it was like a plastic skin. But the marks
on it were photographic, they had not been applied by
hand. The lines were about a quarter of an inch apart
and parallel. The signs themselves were not wedge
shaped but a series of half-moons, dots and short verti-
cals and crosses, vaguely reminding me of Sinhalese
scripts or Sanskrit. Something oriental. I folded it across
the long axis line, eased it under the inside sole of my
shoe, and switched out the light.

When I had replaced the screwdriver I went back
inside and gently stroked Gabby's arm. When she stirred
and turned I said quietly, 'It's almost two o'clock,
sweetie. Time to go.'

I should have liked some warm coffee to start us on
our journey but they would have checked the kettle and
guessed from its heat how long we'd been gone, and
they could draw the net accordingly.

There was very little in our packs, we were wearing
two sweaters each, under our jackets. I pulled the door
to gently behind me and took her hand. Our feet were
naked, for naked feet leave almost no trace on wet grass.
The moon was much lower now and the landscape was

less well lit. There would be two hours of this semi-darkness before the false dawn. I aimed for us to have done seven miles in that time, but only five in the right direction.

Our breath clouded out in front of us as we walked, and gradually our eyes grew accustomed to the darkness. We walked, up to our knees through an icy stream, and I filled our water bottles and soaked the cloth covers to keep them cold. The meadow gave way to hard clay that supported no growth, and then as the first rocks tore at our feet I turned to go higher up the mountain. It took us an hour to scramble up five hundred feet and in the stillness we could hear the incessant roar of waterfalls on both sides of us.

The last five hundred feet took us until the false dawn. Way across on the plains of the Po there would be a glimmer of sun, a trailer, not the real thing. But up here where the waterfalls were thinner only the rock pools picked up an extra lumen from the faint reflection of a reflection. By the time this water had fed its tribute to the mighty Po it would be almost tomorrow. Gabby sat facing me with her bare feet against my crotch for simple warmth. I gave her a smooth, cold pebble to suck. We should need our water by the afternoon and every degree of internal temperature we lost now would take a wicked toll on our bodies to make it up.

I got us moving again, because that last hour before the real dawn was vital. By now we were at least a thousand feet above the cabin, but despite our toil we were now still only level with it.

They would come soon after dawn to catch us as we

slept, and then they would circle the cabin. If they found no trail they would assume I was heading for Milan and the airport, or up towards the frontier. If they found the trail before it petered out on the rock-face it would confirm that we *were* heading north-west for Piacenza or due north to Parma, which both lay on the main road to Milan. From the time we touched the rock the trail would die, even for dogs. Gianni and I had roamed around that kind of terrain for days with hundreds of Germans and braces of dogs hunting us down and we'd watch them flowing back down to the valley each day as night fell. At one stage when we had been particularly irritating near Parma they had pressganged a regiment of Alpini to root us out. They'd dropped their day's rations in little cairns of stones and reported failure to the German commander at Piacenza.

When the first glimmer of the sun came across the mist below us I took a bearing across the valley on the highest place on the opposite range. We were a mile south of the cabin and almost a quarter of a mile up the sheer cliff-face. As the mist rolled slowly down to the valley I could just see the cabin and the last twenty yards of the road as it led off up the mountainside. I planned to stay up the mountain all day, and move down lower during the night. This would give me the chance to watch what they did, and without sight of us for almost a whole day they would widen their net. Early the next morning we would go down to the foothills alongside the road. I reckoned they would take the precaution of putting a man down in Fivizzano and we'd hitch a lift to just short of the town, skirt it on foot, and then with a lift to Aulla I would hire another car and make a dash for Milan, keeping off the main roads.

There was no cover where we were, and I moved us across to where there was a thick mat of last year's brown and rotting bracken. I cut a heap of this and piled it loosely so that we had a small bower that would cover us both sitting up. I left a loose pile at the side of the entrance in case we needed cover from the front. And finally I made a thin clay paste to disguise Gabby's white face and hands.

By six o'clock the sky was blue and cloudless as we ate our cheese and bread, and as we sat at the entrance to the bracken cave I could see the sheep coming up from the foothills to the meadow behind the cabin. I wiped the cheese rind round the lenses of the binoculars, leaving my thumb in the centre. With the lens shields taped forward and only the centre of each lens clear of grease there would be no chance of the sun glinting on the lenses to give our position away.

They came at a quarter to seven. The cars groaned up the track and I heard them stop well short of the top. They were in dead ground from where we were, but they were being very cautious, there was no banging of car doors, and no voices that we could hear. Then they came into sight. There were seven of them. I recognized Monfalcone in a blue tracksuit, Lunghi and his two thugs, and three I hadn't seen before. They walked round our hire car, and as the others walked on one of the unknowns lifted the bonnet and leaned over. He put something in his pocket, pulled down the bonnet and walked towards the others. I guessed our car was missing the rotor from the distributor.

Lunghi and Monfalcone stood at the front door with Lunghi's hoods, and the others went round the back. A few minutes later one of them put his shoulder to the door and they burst in. They were out again in minutes and Lunghi was giving the orders. We could hear the echo of their raised voices now, but not what they said. They were circling the cabin like a disturbed ants' nest. Lunghi and Monfalcone had field-glasses, and they were sweeping over the main road and up the mountainside. They never lifted them to anywhere near our level; they covered the area below the cabin and the pastures below the rock line. Then Lunghi waved to one of his hoods who came over at the trot and stood listening intently. He went back down the path and a car door banged and then we heard it grind its way backward down the pot-holes back to the road.

The others sat in the long grass in front of the cottage and wiped their faces and lit cigarettes. A couple of eager beavers borrowed the glasses and surveyed the countryside. They sat there for two hours, with Monfalcone and Lunghi making trips inside the house. I guessed they were searching to find some clue to what we had been doing there, or where we had gone.

Then we heard the car return and a few moments later we saw Lunghi's man with two others. Each of the others had a German shepherd in tow. They brought out one of the pillows to hold to the dogs' muzzles and then they let them run on long leashes. They circled frantically, noses to the ground, finding and losing scent, and then they picked up the fresh tracks where we had circled the cabin to get to the meadow. For the first fifty yards they pulled their handlers at a headlong rush, but then they were uncertain, casting frenziedly to left and right. A few minutes later they were near the clary and the start of the outcrop rocks and I knew they'd had it. They were standing still with their heads up, ears pricked and their heads looking for movement on the mountainside. But nothing moved. They unleashed them and the dogs circled aimlessly and finally put their noses down on the scent and headed back across the meadow towards the cottage. I could hear the faint echoes of their excited barks and I knew they hadn't a clue. Tracker dogs with effective scents never bark, their tails go up with excitement, but they're always silent.

I heard it before they did, or maybe it was just a feeling in the air, and it came along the valley from the direction of Modena with the sun sparkling on the glossy white paint. It was a small utility helicopter, and as it came nearer I put up our front cover and peered through the fronds of stiff bracken. It was a Hughes 500, designed in the US and assembled in Italy by Nardi, and it clattered slowly overhead, turning about a mile away.

For over an hour it searched the mountainside at hundred-feet intervals, hanging like a lop-sided dragon-fly as the observer trained field glasses on the terrain. Finally it landed in the meadow and I knew that the thrust of the rotors would destroy the last scent of our trail. The pilot and the observer climbed down and walked over to Monfalcone and Lunghi. The observer took off his white helmet and pointed out various sections of the valley. They walked towards the cabin and stopped from time to time so that the observer could indicate with an outstretched arm some sector of search. They went into the cabin and stayed there for about twenty minutes. There was just a slim chance that they were foxing with all the arm waving and pointing to the valley. They could have spotted us from the chopper but it seemed unlikely.

The pilot and the observer came out of the cabin and seconds later Lunghi followed them at the trot. The pilot went first and reached out for Lunghi, and when they'd hauled him in, the observer climbed up and swung the door to. The engine fired, and the rotor blades moved slowly and then caught speed as the pilot angled the blades. It wasn't an easy take-off for a chopper, there was the steep mountainside on their port side and the meadow fell away steeply to the valley. You need to go up very gingerly for the first thirty metres because you're riding on a cushion of very dense air and if you slide off that cushion you drop like a stone and end up with what looks like a wickerwork basket. The chopper sidled towards the mountain and then she went up and out, and dropped a few metres as she hit the hot air from the valley below. Her tail came round and she was away, and she clattered up and down the valley for almost two hours. They hadn't been foxing. They were off our scent and we could take our time and go carefully.

When I looked back at the cabin another car had arrived and two of the men were lifting out a long box. And from the way it was made I knew what was in it. Rifles. As we watched they lifted the lid and each man was handed a rifle and they stood loading the magazines. One by one Lunghi detailed them off and they were spread from the far end of the meadow to the grass in front of the cabin. I pushed Gabby face down and covered her head with my arms. They were shooting at random up the mountainside to see if they flushed anything, and when they were idly searching for targets our heap of bracken would be the only feature on our section of the rock face. The mountain rang to the crashes of the guns and they echoed across the valley seconds later. They were 303s and one would be enough, even at that range. There was the whine of ricochets each side of us as they hit rockface and shattered stones. Then the desultory fire petered out, and we could hear the chopper again. I sat up and looked through our cover. The helicopter was sweeping the other side of the valley and only Monfalcone and Lunghi were still at the cabin.

We ate again and then took turns sleeping and watching. At five o'clock Gabby shook me and I sat up and took the glasses from her. There was another man there and as he turned to point to the hired car I saw that it was Franceschi. And that I didn't like.

He was as used to the mountains as I was, and he knew our little games with the Germans because he'd played them when he was one of Gianni's men. He unfolded a map and laid it out on the gravel drive. From time to time he looked up at the mountainside to check identifiable features. For ten minutes he studied the spread of the mountain and then he was nodding as he talked to Monfalcone. Then they all stood up, brushed themselves down and went into Gianni's cabin.

The light was beginning to go now, there was sunlight across the valley, but with the sun behind the mountain it looked cold and uninviting. An hour later the darkness was everywhere and the sky was dark blue. We stood up and stretched, and I moved our site a short way down the steep slope and over towards a small stream. And that was a mistake.

I planned to move off just before midnight. This would give us ample time to get down to the road, rest, and pick our vehicle for a lift.

We ate the last of our rations at ten and that left only the chocolate. I took over the last watch before we were to move off, and it was only twenty minutes later when I heard it. The chink of metal on metal, the chink of a heavy barrel on a brass button or a sling swivel. Then a stone rolled and rattled only a few feet away to our left. And I could hear him breathing heavily as he came towards us and then he was an extra black shape in the blackness of the night. And then he blocked out a star. I held my breath and put my hand over Gabby's mouth as she stirred.

We must have seen each other at almost the same time, but I'd been alerted and I was already moving as he stood still. My shoulder took him in the belly and I heard him gasp as it went in deep. His gun caught my face as he slid off my shoulder and I felt warm blood inside my shirt collar and the sting of cold air on my cheek and ear. His legs thrashed to put a hold on mine and as my legs bent I reached for the thick neck. But he was on his back and his hands came up to flail at my face and I could smell the pain as he hit my nose, and his breath, as my hand found his windpipe. His legs came across to lever against my groin and as I turned, my thumb went up behind his ear. I moved my hand from his windpipe and both thumbs pressed deep against the join of ear and jaw and I funnelled my body-weight behind my hands and kept it there as the spasms shook his body. It took seconds but it seemed like hours, and when he was still the sweat ran down my face like tears. My arms ached and my thumbs seemed locked and stiff.

I was conscious of Gabby shivering alongside me and I turned the man on his back. It was Franceschi, and in death he looked demonic, his eyes bulging and his lips drawn back in a wide rictus. I turned to face Gabby and her face was white with shock and she was shaking as she knelt with her hands on her knees. Her teeth chattered as she spoke. 'Is he dead, Max?'

'Yep.'

'What are we going to do?'

'We're going to leave him here and make straight for the road. They'll expect him back inside a couple of hours at most. We'll have to take risks, Gabby. I'm sorry.'

She held out her arms to be comforted like a child, and she sobbed as I held her close and stroked the long blonde hair. When it was over I collected our kit and checked the Luger. I went through Franceschi's pockets but there was nothing. Literally nothing. Just like a patrol in the old days. The moon was high and the deep shadows in his eye sockets and his mouth and nostrils made his face look like a skull. But the night air was near freezing at that height, and his body was already stiffening. I crossed his hands and went back to the bracken so that I could cover his face. If it hadn't been for the noise of the stream I should have heard him a hundred yards away and could have moved to avoid him.

I took Gabby's hand because we'd have to move fast and without caution. I struck out diagonally for the road and for an hour it was a nightmare of falling and sliding interspersed with brief rests when the urge to sleep was almost overwhelming. We stood in the shadow of a big outcrop alongside the road, and the air was warm again and there was soft springy turf like balm under our feet.

I let two big saloons pass us and then waved down a farm truck. The driver looked at me with shrewd peasant suspicion, and my appearance can have done nothing to reassure him. But ten thousand lire in notes calmed his fears and he grinned as I called softly to Gabby. He helped us into the back of the truck, and we settled down between the big panniers of grapes and peaches. We kept our heads down as we rattled through Fivizzano and Rometta, and an hour later we were in Aulla. The driver stopped and came round to the side of the truck. He was going to deliver fruit to the hotel by the railway station and he wanted to know where we should like to be dropped. I opted to go with him to the hotel. Although it was not yet five o'clock, the *padrone* was up and about, and servants were vacuuming the entrance hall and the reception area. The cautious *padrone* looked at the two of us in our torn clothes and our unwashed condition but as always the five thousand-lire notes gave us respectability. They also got us breakfast in the kitchen, a wash down for both of us, and a shave for me. As we drank the frothy hot coffee, I looked through the hotel timetable. There

119

was a train at six to Parma, it was an *Accelerato*, which, despite its name, is a slow, local train, stopping at every station. One of the chambermaids walked across the square and bought us our tickets. We walked across and got on the train just before it pulled out.

We had two hours on the train and although I had booked us through to Parma I decided it would be better to get off at Pontremoli. We needed rest and new clothes, and if they traced us down to Aulla they would assume that we'd headed fast for Milan or the frontier at the Brenner Pass.

The Pensione di Napoli made us welcome, and our room was spacious and comfortable, but best of all was the bath. Gabby had first go and I went out to buy new clothes for us both. I bought a morning paper and a small radio, and ordered a coffee at a *trattoria* off the main square. I put the radio to my ear to listen to the news. There were regional bulletins from Genoa, Milan and La Spezia, and then the national news. There was no mention of the events of last night. It was only when I turned to the Second Programme that I realized it was Sunday, as they joined the broadcast from Radio Vaticans. And despite everything the sun shone brighter and my tiredness slipped away. We would stop the world for the day and get off.

Gabby was asleep when I got back. Naked, and relaxed as a cat, she lay across the cotton coverlet on the double bed. The windows were open and the slight breeze moved the strands of blonde hair on the pillow and the sunlight touched her shoulder, and like a broad, bright path it flowed across the globe of one breast, down across the flat, young belly, and lit the golden bush between her legs. There were cuts and scratches on the long, slim legs and the backs of her hands. But for the moment she had peace and I wasn't going to disturb her.

When I'd bathed and shaved I stretched out in the damp towels in the comfortable armchair and I slept for hours. The church bells were clanging and pealing as I woke, and Gabby, who was sitting brushing her hair at the dressing-table, was turned, smiling, to look at me. I looked at my watch. It was midday. I phoned down for a meal and switched on the radio. Dr Kissinger had arrived in Moscow again. The Christian Democrats had been having conversations with the Communists. There had been a warehouse fire in Modena and the usual deaths on the Autostrada del Sole. The temperature would be a few degrees higher than normal for the next three days.

The old lady brought in the tray of food and the big pot of coffee as I switched off the radio. The omelettes were as light as soufflés. When we had finished, Gabby said quietly, 'What do you think they're going to do, Max?'

'You mean when they find Franceschi?'

She nodded.

'They will have found him about the time we got to Aulla. They'll have sent out their hounds up and down the road. They'll have checked garages, car-hire places and probably the station. By now they'll know we're on our way. They won't know where but they'll cover all the possible places.'

'Why did they send Franceschi after us?'

'Because he's the only one who could operate at night in that sort of terrain.'

'D'you think they knew we were there?'

'No. If it hadn't been for the noise of that stream I'd have heard him long before and we could have dodged him.'

'Would he have killed us?'

'Maybe. They seem to be pretty desperate now.'

'Why should they change?'

'I think Lunghi was more important to the Mafia people than Franceschi. I think they used Franceschi to apply pressure to Lunghi because he's essential to them.'

'In what way?'

'Lunghi's the start of the drug line. They need him. I'd guess they're not delivering because they need more cash and Gianni's hoard could save the day. Something like that.'

She looked at me silently for a few moments.

'You worked this out long ago, didn't you?'

'About a week ago I guessed. When I was with Franceschi at Mantoni's place it kind of confirmed it.'

'What confirmed it?'

'Nothing, sweetie. Just instinct.'

She sighed. 'And now what?'

'We'll stay here a couple of days and then I want the other picture from the villa.'

She put her head on one side and for no good reason it reminded me of Tammy. 'Am I a hindrance, Max?'

'No. But I'm going to take you out of the country the first chance I get.' And there was a feeling of barbed wire round the edges of my eyes as two big tears slid down her cheeks.

'You gonna give an old man a last fling, honey.'

She beamed and held out her arms. 'I love you, Max Farne.'

When the bells were thundering away for the evening service, she put a scarf round her head and I walked her across the square to the cathedral. The show had started but nobody frowned as we slid into the back pew. The singing was wonderful and the costumes magnificent. Even in Catholic cathedrals they don't seem to mind too much about you standing up or sitting down in the right places, it's a bit like the last night of the Proms. Gabby lit a candle for Gianni and I bought one for Saint Clare. We walked down to the station and bought two tickets to Piacenza, and two to Modena.

We celebrated the day with a bottle of *chianti classico, piccata di vitello al limone*, and a big dish of small wild strawberries.

Ten

There was a workman's train at seven the next morning that went through to Piacenza. I left Gabby in the carriage and did a recce at Parma. There was nobody I recognized and as we were dressed very differently from when they had last seen us I decided to risk it all the way through to Piacenza.

When we got there I carried the bags of an old lady from our carriage and that made us a party of three. I took tickets to Milan but we got off at Lodi and waited for a bus. We rumbled into the cathedral square in Milan an hour later and took a taxi to the via Jacini near the north railway station. Gianni's villa, or what was left of it, was on the Lecco road and just north of Monza, and I reckoned that Monza was an ideal place to make my base. It was a quiet town and used to the thousands of visitors to the car-racing circuit. You could disappear into this sort of background easier than in a big city or a village.

We had a meal, did a bit of shopping and took the bus. Half an hour later we got off at the Largo Mazzini and I parked Gabby at a restaurant opposite the Santa Maria-in-Strada. I hadn't been in Monza since 1943 but it wasn't much changed and I found the place I was looking for at the back of the old town hall. A neon sign had replaced the old one but it still said 'Hotel Matteo'. There were geraniums in the window-boxes and a boy sat reading a comic on the top step, his hand carelessly but lovingly resting on a dog's head. As I approached, the big black and tan German shepherd eased himself up, ears pricked and eyes watchful. The small boy tore himself away from Asterix and looked up at me. I asked him quietly, *'C'e Signor Mac?'*

He nodded. *'Si signor. Al' cucina.'*

I walked into the small hallway, past the reception desk, down a short corridor and through the double swing doors at the end. Leaning over the big table was a chef in white overalls and standing alongside him was a short, stocky man with a raw-looking face and a tam o'shanter perched on his head. He was reading from a list as the chef checked over the pile of shopping on the table. As the doors swung to behind me the short man looked up for a second, held up his hand to silence me and looked back at his list and went on reading out the items. When he was finished he put down the paper and signed it with a pencil. Then he looked up at me and jerked his head in interrogation.

'Cosa c'e?'

I looked back at him smiling because he hadn't altered. The eyes still held you off and the whole stance of his body was aggressive.

'Mi bisogna due camere per favore.'

'Va bene. Andiamo signor.'

We were walking down the corridor. I was just behind him. 'How're things, sar'n major?'

For a moment he carried on walking, then as the penny dropped he wheeled round and we both stopped as he looked at my face. 'My God, Mr Farne, I didn't recognize you.' And he held out his knobbly hand. 'You don't look different. Apart from the grey hair. It's been a long, long time.'

'I need some help, Mac.'

'Let's go to my office.'

We went up to the first floor and he opened the door of a small room. Everything was so orderly, so neat. Bills on spikes, and neat rows of box-files. Some mail on the old-fashioned desk and on the wall a print of an officer of the Black Watch in full fig. He sat down at the desk and waved me to the chair opposite as he leaned across to pick up the phone. He looked at me with those washed-out blue eyes. 'Tea or coffee?'

'*Cappuccino*, Mac, if you do them.'

He gave the order and hung up. Then he leaned back in his chair.

'How can I help?'

I told him the facts right back to last year. He had known Gianni Podoni because he'd been dropped not long after me and had been responsible for weapon training not only for Gianni's partisans but groups as far away as Florence and Siena. He'd been neat and tidy even then, and the scruffy partisans had never been able to make top nor tail of him.

He had always talked of opening a hotel after the war, but all the same I had been surprised when I got a note in 1946 to say I was always welcome at the Hotel Matteo in Monza. It had been a regular meeting place for partisans, and there had been a radio in the loft and Stens and ammunition in one of the water tanks in the back yard.

The proprietor then had been a fat, jolly Calabrese who made a bare living in those days of food shortage and rationing. The Germans had shot him and ten others in front of the cathedral in 1943. Not because they had found the arms and ammunition, or the radio, but because he happened to be on his way back from bell-ringing at Santa Maria when they were rounding up hostages to shoot in reprisal for the sabotage of the bridge on the Lecco road. He hadn't even been religious. He just liked ringing bells. Every 3 July all the bells in Monza rang out to honour and remember the victims of their gallant former allies.

The old boy had left a widow and a sixteen-year-old daughter. Mac had taken instruction to become a Catholic and then married the young daughter.

When I'd finished telling him my tale of woe he had turned away and gazed out of the window, saying nothing. His two big hands were on the table, clenched into fists, and the big bony knuckles looked like some driftwood smoothed by countless tides into misshapen clubs. Eventually he looked back at me.

'Did you see the boy on the steps of the hotel?'

'The one with the German shepherd?'

'Yes. He's my grandson, Mr Farne. My daughter, his mother, was killed in a car smash. His father left him with us. He's all my wife and I have got. These people you've got mixed up with are very dangerous men. They kill without scruple, without a second thought. I must ask my wife if she would agree before I say yes.'

And he stood up slowly, and as he was closing the

door he said, 'I shall help one way or another.' And then he was gone.

As I waited for him I thought how incredible it seemed for that man, who had sat on hillsides showing his half-circle of seated partisans how to strip a Sten gun, to be a grandfather now. It seemed a long time ago, but not all that long. And I realized that if I had settled back into a respectable civilian life I should probably have been a grandfather too.

I had been in Santa Margherita the day the Italians called it off with their German allies and London had dropped me money and mail in the early evening. One of the letters had been from a solicitor dated two months earlier. It told me that the petitioner, Jane Farne, had been granted a divorce on the grounds of three years' desertion. And there was a short note from Jane. She was going to be one of the first GI brides. He was an infantry lieutenant from Boston, Mass., and she was expecting to be going to the States with him next month. Next month was last month. It wasn't a great blow, no more than reading in the school magazine that some class-mate had bought it in a Spitfire. A pity, but not much more.

After three years in Europe dodging the Gestapo, things in England seemed like things on the moon. Interesting, but nothing to do with real life. And after three years you couldn't really remember what they looked like. Photographs were no more than identity cards from another world, where a pretty girl was smiling, but somehow she was looking through you, rather than at you. So it wasn't a great tragedy but it did make a difference in the long run. I never found reason to be married again and I was never, now, going to be a grandfather. Not as far as I knew, anyway. I realized too that I couldn't even remember Mac's name.

The door opened and he walked round his desk and sat down. 'She says we are to give you all the help we can. Where's the young lady?'

'Thanks Mac. She's at the restaurant next to the jeweller's in the piazza.'

'Well, you fetch her and your kit, and we'll have the rooms ready for you by the time you get back. There'll be no need for you to register as you're friends of the family. That'll make it harder for them to use the police to check.'

Walking back to the square I wondered what there was except wars that could forge such lasting relationships from such tenuous contacts. By treating us as family guests they would be giving us invaluable cover but committing themselves to us in a way that could bring disaster on their heads if Lunghi and his crew traced us to the hotel. There must be great solidarity in a family that could do that. There was no real war-time indebtedness on either side. Just that we had once played dangerous games dressed in the same uniform.

There were a couple of local lads eyeing Gabby from the bar and their disappointment when I turned up was a joy to see.

It took us fifteen minutes to wander along to the hotel, and Mac was waiting for us. He took us up two floors using the back stairs, and the rooms were away from the main corridor down a couple of steps and there was a sign which said 'staff only'. He opened the right-hand door of the two doors that stood side by side and waved us inside. There were two rooms and a bathroom, and they were sunny and clean and homely. Mac stood there as we looked around and then he said, 'Can I have a word with you, Max?'

I went into the corridor with him and he adjusted one of the pictures on the wall to hide his embarrassment.

'I can't do more than this, Max. Just give you a place to be.'

'That's all we need, Mac. I'm very, very grateful.'

He nodded, and as he turned to go he said, over his shoulder, 'Let me know when you want to eat and I'll have it sent up.'

We settled our few things in the drawers of the old-fashioned chest and Gabby lay on the bed and watched me as I stripped down the Luger again. I had the feeling that I was going to need it in good working order. There was one thing I was dreading. The fact that there was no mention of Franceschi's death on the radio news meant that the police weren't involved. That meant they were sure they would get us themselves, without using their police contacts. With the police after us as well we should have a very thin time.

When Mac had gone I stepped out into the corridor and lifted one of the pictures from its hook and brought it back into our room. I put the thin film between the cardboard backing and the painting, and replaced the picture on its hook.

I phoned down to the reception desk and ordered some food. It was Mac's wife who brought it up to us and she introduced herself as she arranged the tray on the small table. When she had finished she stood up. I wouldn't have recognized her. Not that she'd aged badly, her skin was smooth and her face only faintly lined. But her eyes showed the times she had lived through. They were eyes that had seen too much suffering, from the time when they had carried back her father's body from the square. I'd seen the same kind of eyes on policemen. Not unkind, but expecting nothing good from a world they understood all too well.

She spoke very gently.

'He's delighted, you know, to have an old comrade staying here. The partisans helped him a lot after the war, especially in the early days. But your own countrymen, that's what he misses. He's never said anything, but I can tell.' She smiled and slowly wiped her hands on her pinafore as she looked at me.

'You won't let him come to any harm will you, *signor*?'

I shook my head. 'I'm just another guest, *signora*. There need be no connections. But we're very grateful all the same.'

'These people are like wild animals, Signor Farne. Always suspicious, lifting their noses to the wind. They would see a connection just because you and he are English!'

Then, as if dismissing the subject and the danger, she turned to Gabby.

'We were sorry about your papa, my dear. I used to see him sometimes when I was a little girl, and he came here for meetings. A very handsome man, a laughing man, we all felt safe when he was around, and he was not much older than you are now. And he sent us money when the Germans killed my father. He made the new government give Mama a medal when it was all over,

I've still got the piece from the paper when they gave it to my mother. I'll show it to you.'

Like me she noticed the tears waiting to fall, and she put out her hand to touch Gabby's shoulder.

'How about you come with me to church tonight and we light a candle for him?'

She turned to me. 'And we'll say a prayer for you, Signor Farne. I remember what my mother used to say – "when all else fails – maybe a little prayer will help". Is it all right for us to go to church?'

'It's a very kind thought, *signora.*'

It was crazy, but I wasn't going to say so.

While they were at church I walked down the back streets towards the edge of the town. It was still there. No bigger, no brighter than it used to be. Even the sign was still a hand-painted scrawl – 'Auto Biffi'. The big double gates were open and a small boy was throwing stones at some rusty forty-gallon petrol drums. They looked as if they'd been there since the war. I called to the boy, *'C'e Signor Biffi?'*

'Si signor ala casattina.'

And he pointed to where a small building abutted the far side of the workshop. There was no proper pathway to the cottage, just a line where the tall nettles had been cut and trampled aside.

I knocked on the blue door. There was a gramophone or a radio playing inside, and a man's voice was accompanying the music. It was a strong voice and passionate, as its owner sang *'Parlez moi d'amour'* with a heavy Sicilian accent. At the first lull I knocked again. The door opened and he looked much the same, except for the white streaks in his hair. He was a short, stocky man in blue overalls that were patched with grease and a Cortemaggiore dragon on the pocket. He had a piece of paper in one hand and the other held the door open. His eyebrows were raised in query.

'*Io voglio comprare una machina.*'

'*Certo signor, andiamo vedere. C'e un Topolino, una mille cento e una Lancia Aprillia di sessante nove.*'

And he closed the door behind him and waddled across to the workshop. He reached for the light switch and the strip lights flickered and came on. Unlike the surroundings the workshop was neat and clean, with tools on peg-boards and Dymo labels under the specials. The three cars were next to the sliding doors and he gave me a little pitch for each one, patting their bonnets as if they were horses.

I asked him if he would buy it back in a few weeks' time and he grinned as he looked at me. Then the grin faded and he frowned. There must have been something in my accent because he looked hard at my face and said, '*Porca madonna.*' A rather nasty Italian blasphemy. His stubby finger jabbed towards me. 'You're the Englishman – Podoni's friend. What in hell you doing here?'

'Selling boats and taking a break.'

He stood, hands on hips, his head on one side looking me over. 'I remember now,' he said, nodding his head in confirmation. 'There was an Englishman around when Podoni was killed last year. That must have been you.'

'It was.'

He scratched the grey stubble on his chin with a grease-ingrained finger. 'You won't sell many boats in

Monza, *amico*. This is Ferrari country. And it's not much of a place for a holiday either.' The grin was neutral but it demanded an answer.

'Biffi, you were the best transport man the groups ever had. I want an inconspicuous but reliable car. So I've come to you. I'll pay you over the odds but I suggest we leave it at that.'

'How much you prepared to pay?'

'Whatever you ask. I'm not haggling.'

He whistled softly through his teeth as he looked out at the yard.

'You need to carry anything?'

'Could be.'

He walked past a Lancia that was up on a lift and ducked under the front wheels. I followed him and he was pointing at a grey Fiat van. On the side panel were illustrations of ornate bouquets and two obese cherubim of indeterminate sex flanking a text that said 'Fiori di Monza'.

'The florist went off with one of his girls and he paid what he owed me with this van. It's in good order and it's cheap. I could go over it for you in two, three hours.'

'How much, Biffi – in US dollars?'

'*Mamma mia* – let me do my sums.' He grinned. 'I'm not used to real money.'

He did some calculations with a piece of chalk and a lot of noughts on an old cylinder block.

'Half a million lire, or four hundred dollars. But if you want me to buy her back it'll be in lire.'

'How much to tune her up?'

'Thirty dollars.'

'When can I have her.'

He looked at his watch. 'Three hours.'

'Tonight at ten be OK?'

'A bit tight, but OK.'

I gave him the money and he counted it carefully. 'I can't do the documentation until tomorrow.'

'Let's not bother.'

He shrugged and grinned. 'OK *signor*. If that's what you want.'

As I got to the door I turned and said, 'Why the French song, Biffi?'

He looked puzzled for a moment and then laughed. 'I'm learning the language, *signor*. The florist's wife. She's from Paris. A bit of singing cheers her up.' He grinned and reached for a plug spanner from the wall.

When I got back to the Hotel Matteo, Gabby was playing cards with Mac's wife in our bedroom. Gabby was sitting on the bed, her chin resting on her drawn-up knees and her blonde hair in a long pony tail. It seems that they'd lit a giant candle for Gianni and had had words with St Jude on my behalf. I gathered on enquiry that St Jude was in heavenly charge of earthly balls-ups. O ye of little faith.

Biffi had the van ready. He hadn't got a petrol pump but he filled her for me and gave me a spare five litres in a can.

It was going-home-time for all those who had gone up to the lakes for the day, and the traffic was heavy. That suited me fine. I headed down the road to Milan and then pulled off the road at a restaurant. I had a beer and a sandwich and then headed back the way I had come. Nobody followed and I skirted Monza and kept on the main road. I saw the side road to Gianni's villa just in time and turned off and doused my lights. The next twenty vehicles whizzed past without even a glance and I watched their rear lights until they disappeared into the darkness.

There was bright moonlight and I drove without lights down to the big gates. Or at least where the big gates had been. Somebody had smashed the hinges out of the wall and taken the gates away. They had been beautiful wrought-iron work. Black, with gilded decoration. I parked the van in the shadow of the wall inside the gates.

There were deep ruts as I crunched my way down the gravel drive, the spoor of heavy vehicles. They must have started clearing away the debris. When I got to the skeleton of the house I could see that the front wall no longer lay across the drive, there was just a two-foot-high jagged line of cement blocks that marked out the original shape of the villa. There was a pile of window frames where the front door had been and on the far side, away from the villa, was a vast heap of wood. Lath and plaster, panelling and shelving in a huge pyre ready for burning. Beyond the wood was a yellow structure and I walked over to look. It was a diesel shovel and alongside was a row of builders' rubbish skips. There were eight of them and they were all empty. All the masonry had gone.

I lit a cigarette and sat on the step of the digger, thinking. And as I sat there I read the big black letters on the side of the digger. It said 'Escavatore diMaggio – via Pinza, Milano'. I stood up and walked to the end of the digger to where steel steps came down to about three feet from the ground. I clambered up and into the cabin. Alongside the controls was a rack of tools, and hanging from the rack was what I was looking for. A clipboard and a wadge of printed forms.

I sat on the seat and read them carefully. They were handwritten carbon copies and some of the details were illegible but the addresses were there. The papers were instructions for disposal of the various loads. All the masonry rubble was to go to a building site just outside Monza. I'd seen it as I drove up the Lecco highway.

It took half an hour to get there and I left the van well away from the site. There could be locals who might recognize the van, and remember where they'd seen it.

The site was spread over half an acre and they were still at the levelling stage. Apart from a long, wooden site-hut there was very little material or machinery but there were seven or eight mounds of rubble alongside a big bulldozer. I saw the stuff from the villa, it was the only white material there and it looked very small to be all that was left of a house. An hour later I found the slab of wall and half the door frame. There was no picture.

As I walked back towards the site entrance I saw a motorcycle turn off from the road and head towards the site. As its headlight bounced up and down from the rough track it shone directly at me. I went on walking and as I got to the site-hut the motorcyclist arrived too.

He was a tall, thin man and as he took off his crash helmet I could see that he was bald. He pulled the motorcycle up on its bipod and as he walked over to me I decided to dive in at the deep end.

'Good evening. I wonder if you could help me. Who's in charge of the site?'

The big brown eyes looked me over and when he spoke his voice was that of an educated man.

'Maybe you should explain what you are doing here. This is private property. There's a big clear notice at the door that says so.'

'I came to look for a picture.'

He smiled. 'This is a building site *signor*, not a gallery.'

'I understand. But the picture was on the wall of a friend's house that has been demolished. I know the remains have been brought here.'

'What was the house?'

'The Villa di Roma.'

'You'd better come inside.' And he pulled out a bunch of keys and unlocked the door of the hut, and switched on the light. There was a wooden table, a filing cabinet, and a plan chest with rolls of drawings on top. He took off his jacket and hung it on a hook.

'Now then,' he said. 'Tell me more.'

'There's nothing much more to say. There were two small paintings on the wall that I would have liked to keep.'

'Why now?'

'I'm sorry, I don't understand.'

'Why didn't you keep the pictures before the building was demolished? Or before the material was brought here?'

'I wasn't in the country then.'

He looked at me doubtfully and then said, 'Can you describe the pictures?'

'I can describe one of them. They were water colours

with Indian ink. About eighty by twenty centimetres. On cartridge paper, and one was of a fireplace in a mountain cottage with antique pikes over the mantelpiece.'

'Valuable?'

'I wouldn't think so. Pleasant, but not valuable.'

He nodded. 'You weren't the owner?'

'No. He's dead. These belong to his daughter.'

'You've got an accent. What is it? English?'

'Yes. Maybe Scots.'

He smiled and half turned and pointed at a cardboard box beside the filing cabinet.

'Have a look in there.'

There were ornate door-knobs and finger panels. Gilt door-furniture and window catches, hand-painted china drawer knobs and a small pile of broken glass that had cascaded from four pictures stuffed along the side of the box. The first one out was the one I wanted but I took the others out too. The glass had cracked or fallen out in all of them where some charmer had smashed his heel against them. You could see the marks on the cracked glass and on the paintings where the glass had come out.

I picked up the pair and held them up. 'These are the two pictures. Can I offer a reward for them?'

'That's not necessary.'

'Is there something I could send you from England?'

He looked up quickly, smiling.

'Ah, now you tempt me.'

'What?'

'A Palgrave, a pocket edition maybe.'

'Can you write down your name and address for me?'

He searched around for a scrap of paper and wrote on it carefully. 'Professore Giussepe Bonnetti, Universita di Milano.'

He smiled at my surprised look. 'I do a little moon-lighting to earn more money. One of the problems of inflation, you know.'

'I'll send it on to you when I get back.'

He smiled and nodded and opened the hut door for me as if I were a guest at a four-star hotel.

I was back with Gabby in twenty minutes. She slept on while I fiddled with the picture. As soon as I saw the second piece of film I knew what it was.

A page of handwriting had been photographed twice, once with the bottom half of each line stripped over and then with the top half covered. The two separate photographs could be slid together so that the original words could be read. The film from the cottage in the mountains was the top half.

There was no date on the page, and no address. It just said:

> Everything is the property of my daughter Gabriella Maria Podoni, living at the Villa di Roma just off the Lecco highway north of Monza. Twenty per cent is to those who make the arrangements. Lunghi has been given the lead. The syndicate has deposited the cash in account L41017 Banca di Roma, via Gramsci. Pass-book with syndicate goods at via Alfieri 72. The concierge cannot help and is not informed.
>
> The people in Roma will decide future organ-ization. This already agreed by me in case of

emergency or my death. Disposition of property and business concerns by agreement to include my daughter, as laid down in my legal testament of November '69 with Avvocato Cariani.

Giovanni Podoni

As I took my fingers away the two films slid apart, no longer a message, no longer part of the world.

I suppose Gianni must have written notes like that many times, to leave behind some semblance of order if he died. And when you've written two or three that were never needed you probably write the others as part of a routine. You never expect that the one you are writing will be used.

Gianni's writing was regular and firm, and only the signature had the trace of a flourish. I noted the address in the via Alfieri and the bank account number. The syndicate must have gone berserk when Gianni had died in the middle of a deal with the payment irrevocably stuck in the bank's vaults, and the goods and the money in an unknown hiding place. No wonder they'd put such pressure on Franceschi and Lunghi. They only used bank vaults when big money was involved.

I put a match to the corner of one piece of the film and there was a revolting acid smell as it burnt with a swirl of brown smoke. The second piece was damp and it took two matches before the ash floated down into the toilet. I flushed the bowl and waited, and flushed it again, until there was nothing left.

Eleven

I told Gabby to pay our bill and pack our things while I was away. I wanted her to be ready to leave in three hours' time. I went out and bought her a paper and a copy of *Oggi* to pass the time away.

It was just after nine when I parked the van near the Piazza Gramsci and I walked slowly down to the via Alfieri. Number 72 was one of those odd buildings that looks as though it's been squeezed in between two big buildings just to keep them apart. It was three storeys and a basement; one of those buildings that looks as if it doesn't want to join the hubbub of the world. The shutters were closed on all the windows, and although the door was beautifully polished it looked as if it hadn't been opened since it was built. And it was beautiful enough to have been built at least two hundred years ago.

There was a *trattoria* further down the street on the opposite side, and I sat at one of the outside tables with a *cappuccino* and a cigarette. I watched number 72 for twenty minutes but nothing happened. The green shutters stayed shut and the polished door never opened.

There was a knocker in the central panel and on the wall alongside a hanging wire for a bell.

I paid, and walked across the street and stood at the big door, and pulled the bell-wire. I could hear a bell ringing down an empty hall. I knocked with the knocker and saw that it was another of those sea-horse motifs, just like the ones on the gates of Gianni's villa, Lunghi's cuff-links and Monfalcone's tie. The club. The boyos. The syndicate.

And as I stood there the door opened slightly. Two big chains hung across inside and an old lady in black stood there, her eyes looking at my chest. When I spoke her eyes lifted to my face. They were the sad, blind eyes of a glaucoma sufferer and she'd got my height from my voice. I asked her if I could come in, and I said that I'd come on Gianni's instructions.

Slowly, uncertainly, she slid the chains from their hooks and lifted her arms until her hands touched my face. She let her fingers trace the shape of my bones, the line of my hair and the convolutions of my ears. They fleetingly touched my eyes and my mouth. All this time she had uttered no sound. She let her arms fall and she stood back a little.

'What is it you want, *signor*?'

'I want to carry out Signor Podoni's instructions. I want to go up to the apartment.'

The washed-out eyes looked at me as if they could see.

'Signor Podoni is dead, *signor*.'

'I know, *signora*. That's why I am here.'

She stood hesitating for a moment, her head lifted like a wild animal's, scenting the wind for danger. Then she stood aside and bowed me inside. She closed the door behind me and reached behind a curtain, and pointed up the stairs with the key before she handed it to me. Putting her hand under mine and laying the key in my palm as she folded my fingers over it.

Everywhere was spotlessly clean and polished despite the fact that there was nobody to praise or criticize. At the top of the stairs I called down to her.

'*Signora.*'

'*Si, signor.*'

'Has anybody ever been here except Signor Podoni?'

'Nobody. Just the *signor* himself.'

'How often did he come?'

'Sometimes once a week for an hour or two. A few times for the night.'

'And nobody with him.'

She shook her head. '*Nessuno, signor.*'

The key slid easily into the lock and turned smoothly. The room was dark except for a little light from the slats of the shutters at a window on the far wall. I moved my hand round in the darkness for a switch and found two and turned them both and the room was well lit.

It was a long, narrow room that ran full width from the door to the far wall and half that width from the door, backwards over the landing. The floor was of lacquered cork tiles, and the whole room reminded me of a well-designed ship's saloon.

There was no large furniture, and the only seating was a long shelf down the main wall with fitted foam cushions. The walls were soft red mahogany and the light fittings were of brass and white glass. In the narrow part of the room was a small mahogany or rosewood table with one single upright chair.

Just inside the main section there was a spiral staircase of cast-iron, beautifully fretted, and painted white. It led to a small L-shaped balcony rather like a minstrel's gallery. I walked up the staircase and there was a line of photographs on the longer wall. There were two pictures of Gianni's mother. One, in sepia, when she was young. A chubby, serious-faced girl with her hair piled high. The second was taken in a garden somewhere, and she sat holding a bunch of marguerites across her lap. She had one plump hand on a nondescript cat that glared from its place beside her on the wooden bench.

Next there was a picture of Gabby's mother, a formal studio portrait that emphasized the big, soulful eyes and the generous mouth. It was undeniably her, but it was a dream-girl seen through a soft-focus lens. Adjoining it was a photograph of a group of men. Some standing, some sitting. It looked like some Cartier Bresson *opus* from the Spanish civil war. But it wasn't, it was from World War II and from its soot and whitewash harshness, young men smiled as they loosely held Stens or rifles. And one of the young men was Gianni, and one of them was me. Every one of us was smiling, but as I looked it seemed the saddest picture I'd ever seen. We thought we knew so much, and what we were doing was going to make the world all right again. What a naïve, romantic generation to make such a mess of it all.

There were two more photographs. One was of me, squinting into the sun with one eye closed and a silk scarf at the throat of my battle-dress blouse. The last was a picture of a girl. I don't know who she was, but she was breathtakingly beautiful with long, black hair and a smile like a toothpaste ad.

There was a shelf at working level across the short wall, under the shutters that faced the street, and a chair tucked under the work-shelf. Ranged along the work surface was a writing pad, a jar with pens and pencils, an ex-army compass and one of those fold-over leather photo-frames. It was spread out, and upright, like some church triptych, and all the pictures were of Gabby. As a baby, as a toddler, and as a schoolgirl.

There was a wrought-iron railing around the top of the gallery and six or seven rungs of a straight ladder were fixed to the wall. I stood back and looked up. There was a square cover that obviously led to a loft.

I went up hand over hand and then leaned back and thrust at the cover. It went up smoothly and easily, and a light came on above me as the cover fell back on its hinges. It was a fair-sized loft area but only half had been boarded over. There were six metal boxes each about three feet long by two feet square, and a fine layer of grey dust lay on them. They'd been there some time. Except for the marks made by me there was no other disturbance. Nobody had been up there since the boxes were brought up. On top of the nearest box was a green-covered pass-book with the symbol of the Banca di Roma. I slid it into my inside pocket.

The boxes were made of aluminium with close-fitting lids. And beneath the lids there was a thin metal skin, and a welded seam that ran round the four sides of the box. They reminded me of those war-time overseas issue tins of fifty cigarettes. I jabbed in the spike of my ship's knife against the seam, but it didn't pierce the metal. Sometimes welds are stronger than the original material so I used it like a pick on the top surface. The metal was thin and it buckled but wasn't pierced. I jabbed again at the same place and there was a noise like an aerosol spray. The boxes had been vacuum sealed. I turned back a six-inch flap. It was what I had expected. Tight-packed rows of small plastic bags of white powder. It could have been sugar or Andrews liver salts, but it wasn't. It was heroin.

The bags were heat sealed too and I eased one out and opened it just to check. It was dry as a bone and it was uncut heroin. In New York it would be worth about two million dollars wholesale. On the streets about twenty times that much. I slid the bag back inside the box and pressed down the metal flap. I closed the loft cover over my head and went back down the spiral staircase. I pulled the door behind me on Gianni's room.

If it had been anything else – cash, gold, diamonds or the like – I'd have done a deal with the syndicate. But not with heroin. In all the world's prisons they keep the murderers and sexual assailánts of children well away from the general run of prisoners. They wouldn't last a week if they didn't. And for me, the heroin boys were in the same category.

If the general run of the public were forced to see the withdrawal symptoms of just one heroin addict it would do a power of good. Some people have a compulsion to put their hands in mincing machines or touch two live bare wires, but at least they can see the danger, and visualize the result of their action. But with heroin there's no such warning. Just that clean white powder and that unexciting name – 'diacetyl morphine'. And the routes in are so pathetic. To prove you're a swinger, to join the club, to find out who you are. And from the little piece of tin foil over a lighted candle to the hurried, urgent tourniquet that brings up a blue vein on your arm to take the ragged needle is a straight short run to disaster.

It doesn't have to be your nearest and dearest before your heart bleeds. Just see one and I'll guarantee you care. The noise like a cracked coconut as a boy smashes his head against a wall to stop the headaches, the long threads of mucus from a pretty young girl's eyes and nose as it hangs down to mingle with the vomit on her breasts before it drips down to the stinking liquid running down her legs. I swear that it doesn't need to be your son or your daughter who is screaming and jerking before you are horrified. Even the peasants who grow the pretty poppies don't see the effect of their vicious crop. But the organizers and pushers of syndicates have seen it a hundred times and they'd let it happen for a dollar.

There was enough heroin in the boxes to fill every mental home, hospital and prison in the United States of America, and that wasn't on. Not even for pretty Gabby. Not even for my own precious hide.

But I didn't want to lose the boat, and that was the snag.

The old lady took the key from me and touched my arm as she opened the street door for me.

I walked back slowly to the van and by the time I slid in the ignition key I knew what I'd got to do. Whatever it cost I'd got to get Gabby away to England.

On the outskirts of Milan I bought a tourist map and a paper, and a mile or so further on I stopped for a meal.

I measured the road distances with a cigarette and added

on 25 per cent for all those bloody mountains. I reckoned I could just about do it. They'd have some sort of watch on the boat but they must be spread a bit thin on the ground by now.

Two kilometres out of Monza I stopped at a cafe and phoned Gabby. I told her to phone Biffi and arrange for me to have six spare cans of petrol and enough for a complete fill. I would pick her up with our kit at the back entrance to the hotel in ten minutes. She seemed hesitant and it momentarily angered me. I'd got enough to think about without going over every detail twice. I hung up and went to the van.

I didn't make it in ten minutes. It was almost twelve. But she was there with our stuff and I slung it in the back. As I slammed the door on my side I asked, 'You fix the petrol with Biffi OK?'

'There was no answer. I phoned several times.'

'Never mind. It'll only take ten minutes or so.'

'Have you seen the paper, Max?'

'Not yet. It's at the back of your seat if you want it.'

'I've seen it already. You bought me one this morning.'

'So what's it . . .?' and I braked as I turned into one of the small side roads. She was passing me the paper. It was folded in half and across the top was a thick, black headline – 'MURDER IN MOUNTAINS – police seek foreigner.'

The bastards had thrown in the sponge and told the police. There was a long piece about the discovery of the body and it had been identified as Franceschi. He was described as a well-known entrepreneur and sportsman, and the police had information that a foreigner had been seen in the local village. The police were checking all stations, airports and frontier-crossing points. The syndicate must have made its own arrangements with the police and we were now fair game for anyone who took a potshot at us. I switched on and eased in the clutch. As we went past the flower shop I saw that someone had heaved a brick through the fancy glass door. Probably the florist's wife. I pulled up just short of Biffi's place. There was a big red Ferrari sprawled half across the entrance. Arrogant sod.

The door of Biffi's cottage was standing open and I headed that way. I was past the big sliding doors of the workshop before the scene registered with me. Biffi was sitting on a kitchen chair by the work-bench, with his legs and arms tied, and blood all over his face. He was near the welding cylinders, and there was a tall man facing him, holding a small stubby gun, and another one bent over him with a handful of Biffi's hair in his grip as he wrenched Biffi's head back and forth.

The joker with the gun was Lunghi and the one putting the curls in Biffi's hair was Monfalcone. They might be bloody marvellous organizers but they were beginners at the rough stuff. There wasn't a look-out and I guessed that the Ferrari must be theirs. And it only had seats for two. Two to one and armed, they'd jumped on Biffi on their own. And the smashed window at the florist's probably hadn't been a brick or the florist's wife. It was these bastards in a mad hurry to trace the van. Somewhere they'd picked up the van description. Maybe they'd had a tail at Gianni's villa.

There were stacks of petrol cans alongside the wall and I crept back from Biffi's front door to the cans. Some were half empty, some had a pint or so, but four were full and that was enough. I put two back on Biffi's verandah for me, and opened the rest.

I poured the petrol against the base of the sliding door and fed it through so that it ran inside the workshop. There were fancy ways I could clobber those two, but I was on my own, in a hurry, and not too amicably disposed. I was looking forward to a bit of my own back.

I moved two of the big packing cases to give me cover, and I took one of the full cans of petrol and stuck it against the sliding door.

Lunghi didn't look to me like a gunman but Monfalcone was different. It might have been a long time ago when he last used a gun himself, but he had those slow-moving eyes that good gunmen have and I didn't aim to take any chances. The first man out wouldn't know what was going on and that would give me my best chance. This wasn't a sporting contest and I was perfectly happy to shoot a sitting duck.

I was slopping a trail of petrol across the sand to my covering packing cases when I heard Biffi scream. I threw a match to the end of the trail, twice it hesitated and twice it seemed to bridge some small obstacle. And then it was two feet from the sliding door.

In the heat of the sun I could see the petrol fumes against the white paint of the door. The ragged flame flickered and then there was a noise like a wet towel flapping or a spinnaker cracking as it took the wind and filled suddenly. The crack was followed by a wonderful whoosh and there were flames five feet high, twisting and billowing with roaring energy. It must be the same inside the workshop.

It *was* Monfalcone who came out first and he was

holding a Thomson like he knew how to use it. His right hand was reaching over for the safety catch as he ran out. He was looking towards the entrance at the road, sideways on to me and he wasn't a good target. The most I'd get were two clear shots because a hose-pipe spray from the Thomson would rip through the packing cases as if they were paper. They were concealment but not protection. Then he turned to call to Lunghi inside the workshop and the first shot tugged his jacket as it ploughed into his back. The second punched his head forward and his arms went out as if he were treading water. The Thomson fell and Monfalcone slowly collapsed, his knees bent and gave, and with his head still forward his body collapsed backwards and he lay on his back, his handsome shoes pointing towards the workshop.

Then Lunghi came out on the run, he didn't even have a gun. I rested my gun arm along the top of the packing case and sighted on his chest. His face was white and his mouth opened with shock as he saw Monfalcone. He had obviously thought that it was Monfalcone who had fired the shots. His head was lifted to look round as my finger started the squeeze on the trigger. Then the full can went up and the flames seemed to wrap around Lunghi and up to the sign across the workshop doors. As he ran his clothes were aflame as if he were some burning effigy. Nothing was going to help Lunghi and I came out from behind the packing cases with half an instinct to try to help him but the reflexes took over and I sighted with two hands and the blow sent him down as I ran forward. He was probably dead before I hit him because he must have been inhaling flame. Anyway he was dead now and small flames crawled over his remains like giant ants.

Biffi was unconscious, with blood coming from his mouth, and there was wet blood on his greasy singlet and across one leg. I lifted his head gently and his eyes came open but he couldn't see me, his eyes were focused way up on the corrugated roof. I let his head fall forward and headed back towards the entrance.

Gabby was reading the paper, still sitting in the van. She hadn't heard a thing, and if she hadn't, maybe nobody else had either. I told her to take our kit from the van and put it in the trunk of the Ferrari, or if it wouldn't open, to stuff it round the back of the seats. And I told her to sit in the Ferrari and stay there till I came.

It took me twenty minutes to bring Biffi round and clean him up. There was a great piece torn from the back of his scalp. No skin, no hair, just a pale pink layer with tiny pinpoints of blood. He was missing five teeth and that was where the blood came from. And they had deliberately broken the little finger on his right hand.

It seemed that somebody had seen me and the van when I'd gone to the remains of Gianni's villa. They'd used their police contact to check the ownership of the van and they had finally got to Biffi. He had given them a description of me but that was all, and he'd shown them the cash I'd paid. They had no knowledge of a partisan connection and they'd beaten him up on the off-chance that he might know where I was staying. He didn't know so he couldn't tell them, but that didn't stop them.

I gave him half the cash I had on me, and as we hadn't made the transfer official the van was still his. I asked him to give me twenty minutes' start before he called the police.

Gabby was sitting in the Ferrari and I slid in alongside

her. I opened the knife and stuck it up under the dash-
board to get at the ignition wires. The black leather split
open and the foam spread out like a wound, and as my
fingers probed for the wires I saw the ignition keys still
stuck in the dash, two bigger keys hanging down from
the ring.

The Ferrari started at the first touch of the button and
I headed for the main route to Milan. I couldn't afford to
take the route I'd worked out previously and we'd have
to take back roads as far as we could.

It took nearly an hour to go round the outskirts of
Milan. There was the *autostrada* to Genoa and a good
main road that was almost parallel but I daren't take
either. The police would have been warned already. I
wasn't sure how far their cooperation with the syndicate
would go, but I had no intention of testing it out.

I turned left at the Porta Ticinesa and headed down
the Pavia road. Despite the good road it took an hour before
we got to the viale della Liberta and then over the bridge.

When we got to the bridge over the Po I followed the
sign to Voghera and it was well past three when we
reached the railway junction outside the town. I parked
in the station yard and we walked to the town centre and
bought fruit and chocolate and bottles of coke, and then
headed back for the car.

The road from Voghera to Godascio was getting us up
into the mountains and at Bobbio we were in the shadows
of the high valley. We stopped to eat at Torriglia and the
sun was warm again. There had been nothing on the radio
either about Franceschi or the others.

Just outside Torriglia we were waved down by a
policeman with a rifle. He had stepped out from the side

of a shepherd's hut and I would have had to drive at him to get past. I got out of the car and he was bending to check the number. The road was quite empty in both directions and I hit him across the throat. He dropped the rifle and it clattered across the bonnet and bounced to the road. I dragged him to the side of the road and went back for his rifle. I slid out the bolt and threw it into the gorse bushes up the slope of the mountains.

If I went straight on they'd have me at the junction above Genoa, and they'd take it for granted that I *would* go straight on. I did a U-turn and we flew back up the road and took the right turn to Neirone. We swept on through Gattorna and San Andrea di Foggia. It was dark now and past eight o'clock. We crossed and recrossed the Lavagna river a dozen times to take country roads down towards the coast.

We hit the coast road just east of the Chiavari tunnel and I prayed a small prayer as we entered Rapallo. I don't know what I prayed for but nothing happened and I stopped near the crown of the hill where we had once been stopped by Franceschi's men. I stashed Gabby in those same olive groves with our worldly goods and got under the Ferrari and jabbed up with the spike of my knife. There was a rust spot at one of the fuel tank welds, and the petrol came gushing out. When it was just a drip I shoved the wheels into position and put her in neutral and leaned over and touched the clip on the brake so that it sprang up, I put my shoulder against the bonnet and she went off smoothly backwards. As she went over the edge the sump touched a rock and sparked but there wasn't enough petrol to burn. I could see her go in the moonlight. The end hit an outcrop, and she turned on her back so that all her underside was exposed like an over-turned turtle. And then she curved over gracefully on her back like a diver and there was a terrible grinding and crashing as she hit the rocks in the darkness below. And then silence, except for the sound of the sea.

I crossed the road and went deep into the olive grove to find Gabby. She was sitting with her head resting on her drawn-up knees, her hair white in the moonlight.

I reached for my small pack.

'Which d'you want? Milk or plain?'

'Milk.'

While she was peeling off the wrapper I said, 'I want you to listen carefully to what I'm going to tell you.'

'I'm listening.'

'We're going to the Miramare at the top of the hill. We shall have a nice meal and then we shall go down from the hotel gardens to the bottom of the cliffs. Then we'll swim, nice and easy, across the bay and we'll wait for the right moment and get on board. I'll cut . . .'

'I can't swim, Max.'

'Never mind, I'll take you to the nearest dinghy and then I'll tow you across. Don't worry. Anyway – I'll cut the ropes and let the boat go with the current and when we're out of range of their pistols I'll start her up and we'll be away.'

'Where to, Max?'

'Eventually England. Maybe France first.'

She put out her hand and touched mine. 'I'm frightened, Max.'

'Of what?'

'Of the sea.'

'It'll be flat as a board, sweetie. I'll just tow you over nice and easy.'

She squeezed my hand but she was trembling. I stood up and held out my hand and pulled her up. I put my arm round her waist and we walked down to the road and turned up the coast road to the top of the hill.

It was further than I thought to the hotel and took us half an hour. I booked us two rooms and there was no problem although they looked a bit sideways because of our lack of luggage and our appearance. But, as always, they took a quick cheerful look at Gabby and an envious, superior look at me, and let us in.

While Gabby was putting herself to rights I went down to the garden. I walked along the top of the cliff and was horrified. Everywhere the cliff dropped vertically. Only at the side of the main road, in full sight of passers-by, was there a slope that we could reasonably use.

I went back over the whole length of the cliff-top. There was one possible way down. There was a crevasse about five feet wide, and the moonlight just touched a ledge about six inches wide, almost nine feet from the top. Below, the rocks gave access to the beach. We could just about do it if Gabby could use my legs and arms as a climbing frame. But I wouldn't give us more than a fifty-fifty chance.

The restaurant was crowded when we went down for a late dinner and we lingered over our coffee, listening to the band and letting the time go by. I checked our stuff. The weapons, passports and money. I went over the details one last time, then I took her arm and we walked through the big french doors that gave on to the gardens.

Twelve

Light flooded out from the ballroom, washing over the terrace until it died at the cliff's edge. We stood in the shadows of the stone pillars that made up the supports of the wooden-framed loggia and listened. Below us was the noise of the sea as it curled between the rocks and sent its salty fingers up the cliff face. Behind us there was the hum of voices and the faint strains of the orchestra. They were playing 'Some Enchanted Evening'. A waiter came out and we watched as he cleaned the tables and tipped chairs on end to keep off tomorrow morning's dew.

Across to our right the lights of the town seemed to flicker as they were hidden and revealed by the leaves of the trees moving in the night breeze. It was too far away to hear the traffic over the rush of the sea but I could see the two cars drawn up at the entrance to the jetty. They blocked the way completely and I could see several men leaning watchfully against the promenade railings. There was a police car by the fish-market with its top light flashing and its headlights on.

I could just make out *My Joanna*. They'd moved her

right to the end of the jetty to the farthest berth from the promenade. I looked at my watch. It was ten past midnight and the moon would be full in twenty minutes. I took Gabby's hand and moved down to the edge of the cliff. The drop to the first shelf looked impossible. It was perhaps nine feet, but even there there was not more than four inches of foothold. I lowered myself over the edge until I was hanging by my fingers and I leaned back and let go. My back hit the other side with a head-shaking force, and my feet slipped as they took my weight. Then I edged down slowly, moving each foot carefully until my right foot eventually touched the ledge. My jacket was corrugated up to my arm-pits but it was protection for my back.

I levered myself forward with both arms, and then, with my feet as a fulcrum, I reached forward with my left arm and with both arms outstretched in opposite directions I could just brace myself. But the stretch was so wide that I couldn't keep both hands completely flat at the same time.

I had told Gabby what she had to do, and I called up to her softly. 'Now, Gabby.' I couldn't even look up to watch her, and then like some circus acrobat her sandalled foot touched my head, found a purchase, and I braced my neck. Then her other foot was on my shoulder, and I pressed with both hands with all my strength and I heard her gasp as she loosed her hold on the cliff top and lowered herself downwards until both her hands were holding on to my left arm, and both her feet were on my right leg. And my arms and legs felt as if they were on fire. Slowly and carefully she used my spreadeagled body as a lattice until she was hanging from the hook of my left foot where it thrust against the rockface. The sweat that poured down burnt my eyes, and I could feel my foot drag slowly downwards with the weight of Gabby's body. For a moment she swung and I saw her blonde hair shine out, fanning out in the moonlight, and then a stone rolled, and bounced, and clattered its way down below us, and almost at once she called up. 'I'm there, Max.' The thought of moving my feet or my arms was torture itself and I remembered that little woman, Mac's wife, sitting on the bed in the sunny room, saying, 'And when all else fails, maybe a little prayer.'

And I prayed my little prayer as I moved one hand. There seemed to be a swath of pain that lay across my arm and shoulder like a heavy yoke, but I moved the matching foot and then again and again. It took ten minutes to get down to the ledge where Gabby waited with white, upturned face, but it felt like a lifetime, a nightmare of deep blue sky, glittering sea, falling stones and my breath fighting its way into my lungs.

She put both her hands up to cup my face as I leaned against the rock and she wiped the sweat from my face and neck as it lay in ice-cold beads on my hot flesh.

It took twenty minutes more for us to clamber down to the sea. I took her hand and walked out till the water was up to her shoulders. I turned her to face me and kissed her gently, and we stood with our arms around each other for a few moments. She needed all the encouragement I could give her. If she panicked we should both be finished. And if you can swim it's not easy to imagine what it takes to walk out into the sea when you've never swum in your life.

I put my hands on the smooth young shoulders and looked at her upturned face. 'We'll be fine, sweetie. It's only a hundred yards to the dinghy and then you'll be out of the water. I'll take the boat over to the jetty and hold her while you get on board. In the dinghy you lie flat and when you get on board *My Joanna* keep to the seaward side and go up to the foredeck. There's a white canister there, a big one, just lie there and do nothing. When the boat starts moving you stay put. I'll come round for you when we're clear. *Capito*?' She nodded. Her teeth were chattering and she was shivering violently. I held out my hands for her. 'Lie on me. Just lie.' And with my hands under her armpits I thrust off.

The sea was warm, thank God, and just a gentle swell from the water fighting the offshore wind. I looked up at the stars and talked to Gabby of some of the constellations we could see. I told her that these same stars would guide us home on our journey back to England. But after a few minutes I needed all my breath for our task.

When I looked behind me we were still on course but seemed to have made little way. It took fifteen minutes before we were at the dinghy. I made her put up both arms as I held her so that she could grab the gunwale. Her hand turned a rowlock in its swivel and the noise seemed like an explosion on our pool of silence. The boat tilted wildly as she clambered in, and I shoved it back upright and held it as she lay down. It sat well down in the water and would be barely visible from the shore at sea-level, and I prayed that nobody would see us from the hotel garden and report a dinghy drifting loose.

I unlashed the unsailorly knots that held her to the white buoy, and her stern swung round even before I got her moving. I held the rope over my shoulder and then fastened it under my arms and round my chest. She came with me easily but she was beam-on to the current, and I had to exert myself to keep her on course. I was aiming for a spot about ten yards out from the breakwater steps.

After half an hour I made what should be the last check. We were too far out. At least twenty yards away instead of ten, and the current was running faster now. In ten minutes fighting the flow I made only three or four feet, and I knew my strength was going. There was nothing to do but take the risk of us drifting out to sea and I swam across the current. Slowly we turned and made progress but away from the breakwater. After ten minutes I felt the cold water. We were way past the breakwater and the cold stream was off the shore. The main current swept down the side of the jetty and out to the sea. Warm from the day's sun and the shallow bay. The cold stream was a flow that missed the current from the shelter of the breakwater. After ten minutes' swimming a pain shot from my ankle to my knee, but it was a welcome pain. My foot had struck the steps below the water. I knocked on the hull and Gabby raised her head. The dinghy was grinding against the bottom step. I whispered to her, 'Get out, rest for a moment, and then go to the boat. She's right there on the corner.' She nodded and I held the boat as she slid over the side.

I loosed the rope and the dinghy drifted slowly stern first till she met the pull of the current and then she was swept out of my sight. I watched Gabby as she clambered up the steps into the shadows.

It took me another fifteen minutes to round the break-water and I could see the glint on the chrome of *My Joanna*'s pulpit. The first rope sheared easily, and the boat's head came round but was held by the for'ard spring. I sliced through the spring and the boat's high bow swung almost six feet away from the sea-wall. As I moved on down the boat I realized that the twin rudders must be set before I let her drift. It took me ten panting minutes, diving without splashing, under the rake of the keel. The rudders came round inch by inch until they were at 180 degrees.

The current was running too fast now for me to risk cutting the last spring and the stern rope. She was tugging at her mooring and with the last two ropes cut the boat could swing off and away before I could board her.

I had to slide between the stern of the hull and risk getting crushed against the sea-wall if she swung back again. The stern rope sagged for a moment and as it tightened I grabbed for it and hung on with both hands. Then I slowly went hand over hand along the rope until I was level with the deck. She started to swing back and I hauled myself up and reached for one of the stan-chions and missed. There was condensation on the chrome and my hand couldn't grip the smooth surface. I had got to risk being seen for a longer time than I had planned.

She came swinging in, and as the rope slackened I hooked my arm round the bottom of the nearest stan-chion and loosed the rope as I brought round my other arm. For a few seconds the boat rode against me with my chest as a fender. I shoved with my feet against the sea-wall and she wouldn't budge. I was held there for several moments fighting for breath and then she swung away again and I clawed my way through the rails and lay flat on the side deck. I was right by the wheelhouse door and I reached up with the key without getting up. It slid in easily but I hadn't enough leverage to turn it. I knelt up and twisted the key in the lock. It turned, and the door slid open.

Inside, I checked the instruments. Fuel was still topped up in both tanks. The batteries showed a 90 per cent charge. The echo-sounder showed 30 feet. I lashed the wheel to a straight ahead course and crawled back on deck. I scrambled round to the foredeck, and Gabby was there, her white face turned to look at me. I put my mouth to her ear. 'I'm going to bring you the mop. If she turns her head towards the jetty fend her off. But don't stand up. Sit and do it.'

I slid the mop along the side-deck for her, and lifted the boat-hook out of its clips for me. I knelt up and looked along the jetty. There were seven or eight figures at the end where it met the promenade and two of them were in uniform. None of them were looking our way but they all looked horribly near. I leaned over and sliced through the spring, and then the stern rope, and gently pushed against the wall with the boat-hook. She came away three feet and I waved to Gabby to use the deck mop and that pulled her head straight again.

I unlashed the wheel and turned the rudders as we slowly slid along. She was six feet from the wall as her pulpit edged past the end of the jetty. The current ran crossways here, as it fanned out to the bay and the open sea. She seemed to move unbelievably slowly but her stern was clear of the sea-wall in five minutes. Then the full force of the main current grabbed us. The rudders wouldn't hold her on a course now, and I brought them round to line up with the drift.

There was a surface breeze too, and the combination sent us skewing away to the west, diagonally and dangerously beam on to the chop that the wind created. There were no vessels that I could see near our course and I peered ahead as we drifted silently. I turned on the switches to warm the diesels and exactly as I did so there was a blinding light from behind us. It filled the wheelhouse and spread out over the afterdeck. I looked behind me and saw a searchlight and then another. The second was sweeping the water on both sides of us. I shouted to Gabby to come inside at the double, and as she closed the wheelhouse door behind us a bullet whined off the port davit and out to sea.

I turned the key to the last notch and the engines came up and I shoved the revs up to 2,000 in neutral. Then back to 750 and into gear, and she jumped forward as I slid both levers forward till we were slowly going up to 3,000. I wanted to clear the three-mile limit as far as possible, as quickly as possible, but running due south I'd have had seven or eight knots of current across me and I needed it with me. I set her with the stream and we must have been making 17 knots. Then a bullet smashed the aft window, and glass showered and tinkled on the teak gratings and another bullet thunked into the coach-house roof. I'd have to zig-zag and lose distance, otherwise they could take pot-shots at us like a sitting duck. They obviously had only one rifle and it was firing single shots. I switched on the radio and turned to Genoa Maritime frequency. There was static but no traffic and I turned down the volume but left the set on.

Gabby swept up the loose glass and I slung it overboard and walked round to the afterdeck. They were firing with a submachine-gun now and tracer was arcing from the jetty to the sea. The tracer was more use to me than them because although, as I watched, they lifted the trajectory, the tracer was clearly falling short of us. I looked at my watch, it was 3.30 a.m.

We had a coffee and I put Gabby at the wheel while I went back on deck again. There were lights on the water near the jetty but it was too far away for me to see what they were up to. But a few minutes later I heard the rasping roar of a speed-boat. I watched her small searchlight head our way and when she was about two hundred metres behind us I saw that there were two men. One was at the wheel and the other was in uniform and he had a rifle across his knees.

Then I heard him on the loud-hailer. The wind carried his voice in snatches across the water. 'Farne – stop the boat – or we shoot' and he made to stand up and level the rifle. He couldn't have hit us if we had been ten times the size.

I went back down to the wheelhouse and took over the wheel. I gave it a series of short, quick turns both sides of our course and looked out through the empty rear window. The light, planing craft was hitting our foaming wake only fifty metres away and it was bucking and plunging like a wild horse.

* * *

They'd send something bigger and better, but we were well clear of Italian territorial waters now, by at least seven miles, and I switched the radio to the marine radio-beacon at La Spezia, and waited. Their call-sign comes up at six minutes past the hour and the half-hour. At exactly six minutes past four it came over – four dashes for TO, and I twisted the DF bar to get a null and noted the bearing. Two minutes later I took the beacon from Genoa on 301.1 kcs and marked it on the chart. We were forty kilometres outside the three-mile limit of Italian waters.

I put the switch over to transmit and called Genoa, and asked them to give us the radio-telephone service. At that time in the morning there were no queues and I got the consulate in a couple of minutes. A languid voice took the call.

'Duty Officer British Consulate Genoa speaking.'

'This is British motor vessel *My Joanna* registered Port of London. Will you note that?'

'What can I do for you?'

'I want my call frequency monitored for the next twenty-four hours.'

'I'm afraid we don't provide such a service.'

'I know you don't, sweetheart. But if you don't do it now that I've warned you, you could be up to your neck in an international incident.'

There was the nearest thing to a minute's silence that you can get on a ship-to-shore call, and then the bored voice said, 'Are you in harbour at Genoa?'

'No, we are at sea.'

'And who is speaking?'

'My name is Farne. I'm the owner and skipper.'

'I see. And your frequency?'

'Channel 21.'

'And what's the trouble, is it . . .?' and the penny dropped. 'My God, are you the fellow who was in that business at Milan yesterday?'

'I am.'

'Well I suggest you head for Genoa and report to the police. You could phone us later on if you thought we could help, old boy.'

'We are not in Italian waters and I don't intend coming back to any Italian port. I'll tell you what I want you to do.'

'You realize that they're after you for murder, Mr Farne; we couldn't interfere.'

'Just wake up the consul himself and tell him to call me through Genoa. In two hours we shall be out of radio contact with Genoa.'

And I hung up.

Gabby got us a magnificent breakfast from dampish corn-flakes, followed by a dried egg omelette, and biscuit with tinned marmalade. We sat naked, with our wet clothes drying on deck as the sun came up. Then the radio crackled and Genoa maritime came on.

'Calling motor vessel *My Joanna*, calling motor vessel *My Joanna*.'

'*My Joanna* here.'

'A radio link with Genoa 56833.'

'OK.'

'Is that Mr Farne?'

'Farne speaking, who is that?'

'This is James Higgins, British Consul Genoa. What's the problem?'

'You have seen the reports of the affair in Milan, Mr Higgins?'

'Yes, I have. Are they true?'

'To some extent. The shots were fired in self-defence by me, and in the protection of a British citizen Gabriella Podoni.'

'I see. I can only recommend that you report to the Italian police, Mr Farne, and maybe we can help you on the legal side.'

'Mr Higgins, I wouldn't trust the Italian police. Not in this area anyway. Half of them are in the pay of the syndicate.'

'I'm sure you are wrong, Mr Farne.' But his voice expressed different sentiments from his words. He knew that we probably had a considerable audience by now.

'I should like you to get in touch with the Italian Ministry of Justice and pass them a message from me.'

'I see. What is the message?'

'Tell them that Monfalcone and Lunghi were the two ends of a drug connection. Monfalcone in New York and Lunghi over here.'

'Can you prove that, Mr Farne?'

'I can tell them where there is a large quantity of heroin that belongs to these people.'

'Have you actually seen it?'

'Yes.'

'And what do you propose to do if they send an official boat out to you? The police maybe, or even the Navy?'

'I'm well outside the three-mile limit.'

'I understand you are a professional sailor, Mr Farne?'

'Sort of.'

'I think you should check your maritime law.'

'I'll give you my position, Mr . . .'

He interrupted. 'No. Don't do that. Just bear in mind what I have said. I suspect you must be somewhere in the Gulf of Tigullio. There's no need to answer.'

'What about the Ministry of Justice?'

'I will make the necessary contact but I shall have to go through the Embassy in Rome. Are you in any danger where you are?'

'No, we're quite safe.'

'I'll call you back.'

As soon as he said 'Gulf of Tigullio' I realized the point he was making. Under International Law of the Sea a country could claim that a bay was home waters from inside a line joining the two extreme landfalls. I sat at the smaller scale chart and pencilled on that line, and plotted our position. It would take us an hour at full revs to get clear of the bay. Even as I put down the dividers I heard a plane. It came in low over the sea. A single-engined job, flat horizontal wings with no dihedral. It swept over us and its outline from below was just like a Hurricane's. I saw with relief the Italian Air Force markings on the wings and the tail, and then I realized what it was – an SIAI-Marchetti 1019. They'd only taken delivery of the first six at the beginning of the year. It banked steeply and came round again. There was a pilot and an observer and they were wearing IAF overalls with rank flashes. They circled us four times and then flew off low over the sea. Probably testing out the surveillance electronics on shore to combine business with business.

It was bang on the hour when I spotted the white hull on the horizon. The sun was reflecting the brilliant white and she was much bigger than *My Joanna*. I re-knotted the Red Ensign and put up French and Italian courtesy pennants on the mast on the foredeck. Then I checked our bearings with the Genoa and La Spezia beacons. We were five miles due south of the line that touched the outlying western and eastern tips of the bay. By my reckoning we were well outside Italian home waters.

I made her shipshape, and Gabby was adding those little feminine touches like getting out the booze and substituting *Penthouse* for Reed's *Nautical Almanac*. I entered our position and DF bearings in the log.

By now the approaching vessel was clearly visible. She was a businesslike patrol boat about 60 foot overall, flying the Italian flag and with that special presence that all navy boats have in peace-time. There was a four-inch gun on the foredeck, flanked by a pair of machine-guns. But all the muzzles had their covers on.

She came in alongside and stood off about twenty feet, and both vessels moved slowly together like a pair of self-confident swans. There was a uniformed officer on deck and several ratings. I went up on deck and the officer used his loud-hailer.

'*My Joanna*, ahoy. I should like to come aboard.'

I unhooked the Aldis and uncovered the lens. If we were going to parley I reckoned that it was best to have the preliminaries in writing. You can easily deny the spoken word, but using Morse meant that it would have to go in their log as well as mine. I flashed 'Who are you? What do you want?'

There was some rushing about on the patrol boat and then they were flashing back.

'Italian naval patrol boat P74. May I come aboard? Capitano Felice.'

'We are in international waters, you have no authority to board.'

'Regret cannot agree. These waters subject to Italian control. Prefer not to use force.'

'We have checked our position with Genoa and La Spezia beacons and are in communication with British Consul Genoa.'

'Your position understood and respected but must carry out my orders.'

'What orders?'

'To board your vessel and take statement and if appropriate arrest your boat and crew.'

'We shall resist.'

There was a lull from the other side and then they were flashing again.

'Suggest that we divide procedure in two parts. May I come on board and discuss situation.'

'Provided you wear civilian clothes agreed.'

'Agreed.'

I broke the chain open that gave entrance to our deck and hooked on the bathing ladder. Five minutes later he appeared, and as *My Joanna* sidled towards the patrol-boat there were four ratings putting down fenders. Their freeboard was not much more than ours and when we touched for a second he jumped across.

He was a big built man, tall and broad-shouldered, and I could tell from the way he stood on the deck that he had been around boats for a long time. He walked forward, hand outstretched.

'Felice, Capitano Guido Felice, Italian Navy. Pleased to meet you.'

And when we had shaken hands he turned and waved to his crew, and I saw the water threshing at his boat's transom as she stood off from us. He turned back and faced me, brown hands on hips.

'Can we talk, Signor Farne?'

'Of course, let's go down to the saloon.'

I introduced him to Gabby and he did the full Italian bit right down to kissing her hand. He was wearing a heavy white sweater, white Navy shorts, long white stockings and issue shoes.

I waved him to a seat alongside the saloon table and Gabby kept the boat roughly on course. We were slowly moving due west and I wondered if he had noticed. And if he had, had he rumbled why.

When I offered him a drink he opted for whisky and I poured us both a measure or two. He sat looking at me with his eyes half closed. Waiting for me to talk. But I didn't co-operate and when the silence was becoming noticeable he took one last swig at the whisky, clamped the glass down on the table and looked across at me.

'We've both got a problem, Mr Farne. Yours is bigger than mine but mine is right here, right now.'

I didn't respond and the thick black eyebrows lifted with just an indication of annoyance.

'There is a judge's warrant out for your arrest, Farne. For murder.'

And the brown eyes looked for a reaction in my face. I stayed very still.

'It's alleged that you were concerned with the killing of two men in Monza and another in the mountains north of La Spezia. The police want to question you regarding these serious crimes.'

He folded his arms across his chest as he leaned back, and I knew that this time he would wait for an answer no matter how long it took. He had that grim, self-righteous look of men who only kill other men with government authority.

'Capitano Felice, first of all I deny the allegations. Secondly I am in international waters and therefore not under your jurisdiction, and thirdly you are the Navy not the police.'

He nodded but he was eager to say his piece.

'I have a police officer on board and you certainly are in Italian waters. You are in the measured area of the gulf of Tigullio.'

'Captain, I have taken bearings just before your arrival, from the beacons at La Spezia and Genoa and they show me seven to ten miles beyond the bay line. The record's in my log.'

He took out a white linen handkerchief and wiped his mouth as if he were also wiping my stupidity away.

'Your readings may be wrong. Logs have been wrong before, especially pleasure boats' logs.'

'I've held a Master's Certificate for nearly twenty years, Captain. So I shouldn't try that one. And as a precaution I have been in touch with the British Consul in Genoa.'

'Have you had customs clearance from Santa Margherita?'

'No, and I wouldn't need it if, as you say, I'm in Italian waters. You can't have it both ways.'

His tongue probed around in the big white teeth as he looked me over.'

'Can I ask where you're bound?'

'To Chichester, Sussex, England.'

'Via?'

'France, Spain and through the Bay.'

He put his hands on the table as if he were going to stand up but the relaxed fingers told me he was bluffing. He lifted his backside a few inches to show willing.

'Well, we shall have to ask the French to extradite you.'

'How long would that take?'

He shrugged, but calmly, his lips pursed.

'Two hours, maybe three.'

'Even with all the publicity?'

He laughed dismissively. 'About one little boat under arrest, Signor Farne?'

'No, about Italians smuggling drugs into the United States.'

It looked like they hadn't heard my radio chat to the consul. Or they hadn't told him. But he did his blustering best.

'There are always stories about drugs in the Mediterranean, Farne. They keep the newspapers happy in the summer dog days.'

'I mean two million dollars' worth of heroin sitting in Milano. And I mean Lunghi was this end of the line and Monfalcone was the New York connection. And I mean that it's a Mafia deal, Capitano. But I agree that it will keep the newspapers happy for months. And the politicians too.'

His thick fingers were doing arpeggios on the table-top and he was looking hard at me, trying to work out the implications.

'Where is this heroin?'

I smiled. 'With respect, Captain, I've no intention of telling you.' I held up my hand as he opened his mouth to speak. 'But I am prepared to give a full statement to your embassy in London after I get back.'

His hand slammed down on the table.

'You must be mad, Farne. You are wanted for murder.'

I stood up and put the cork in the whisky bottle so that he'd get the message.

'You said you wanted to talk, Captain. We've talked.'

He stood up, hitching up his shorts.

'I'll have to place your boat under arrest, Signor Farne. I have no alternative.'

'I'll see you back to your boat, Capitano, and after you are aboard her if she comes within twenty feet of this boat I shall open fire in self-defence and put out an international SOS that I am being attacked on the high seas.'

Even to me it sounded a bit overdone, but it was what I would do and a touch of 'Rule Britannia' brightens up even the Proms.

'I can jam your transmissions.'

I laughed. 'If you jam anything on 2182 you'll have every government in Europe on your neck, not to mention the NATO fleet, the US Fifth Fleet, plus the Egyptians and the Israelis. No, I shouldn't do that, Felice.'

He stomped his way up to the side-deck and he held the grab-rail as he waved for his boat to come alongside.

Even hard pressed as he was he kept the courtesies of the sea and just before he jumped he shook my hand briefly.

I locked back the chain and watched as the patrol boat sheered off and Felice went through the saloon door. I wouldn't fancy being at the other end of his radio call. He was tough all right but they had only given him half the story. Or maybe they hadn't monitored my early morning call to the consul.

I went through the deck locker and found what I was looking for, and spread the white canvas out on the afterdeck and checked the nylon ropes. They were two drogue anchors that I hadn't used for over a year. Drogue anchors look like heavy parachutes and skilfully placed they can pull down the drift of a boat to next to nothing.

With only Gabby and myself on board I reckoned that Felice would expect us to be exhausted from lack of sleep very soon. He would already know that we hadn't slept for twenty-four hours and he would assume that we should have to take turn and turn about steering the boat during the night. And after a day of this, or maybe two, he would think that we should be ready to call it a day.

On the port side, opposite the steering wheel, was a gimballed compass and below it was a plain teak panel. The panel hinged down if you had the key, and behind it were the three control panels of the auto-pilot. Visitors to boats find knobs and switches irresistible, and the auto-pilot has sixteen knobs and three switches, so it pays to keep them out of sight. It can take three hours' hard work resetting the controls, and anyway, hydraulic controls don't take kindly to knob-twiddling. With the drogues cutting down our speed to a couple of knots the auto-pilot could keep us on course for hours and I could cut one engine and save fuel.

It took an hour to sling the drogues and adjust them so that they streamed well clear of the screws and the rudders. I could see Felice watching through big night glasses.

I took bearings again from Genoa and La Spezia, and marked off our position on the chart. We were not only well clear of Italian waters in a southerly direction but we were far beyond the most westerly feature of the bay itself. International waters would be measured now from the coast itself. By the morning, even at a slow drift, we should be almost due south of Genoa and with the drogues pulled in for the day we should be due south of the coastal frontier between Italy and France by mid-afternoon. And that would give the Italians another little problem.

I killed the port diesel and started adjusting the trim on the auto-pilot. That took an hour, and while I worked Gabby got us a meal, and I ate while I worked. The gears had started a hunting action and the right and left audio signals were pinging away like church bells. I suppose the auto-pilot wasn't used to the inertia of the drogue anchors. Neither was I, but I tightened some slack on one of the drive chains and that seemed to cure it.

By now it was dark enough for the navigation lights, and I switched those on and the pink-shaded lamp on the saloon table. The last job was to tack two layers of canvas across the gaping hole where the aft window had been.

On the patrol boat the lights were all on and the searchlight on top of their wheelhouse was on. They were at least fifty yards away but the white light washed over our davits, the dinghy, and the whole of the after deck, with an eerie white light that cast long shadows across the water on our starboard side.

Even without the glasses I could see the foam at the patrol boat's stern. We were going so slowly because of the drogues that the bigger boat was having to go ahead and astern every few minutes to keep on station. It must be driving them frantic and it was certainly putting up the temperature in their engineroom.

I was drawing the curtain across the saloon windows, and they must have been waiting to catch my eye because their Aldis was winking and blinking urgently. I reached for the pad and pencil and turned our Aldis towards them and told them to go ahead.

Their signal was short and to the point.

'Motor vessel *My Joanna*. Am instructed to arrest your ship and crew. Request you follow me. Will escort you to port of Genoa. Felice Captain.'

I reached across and cranked the radio round to 2182 and lifted the phone off the hook. And then I jiggled away on our Aldis.

'Motor vessel *My Joanna* to Italian Navy patrol boat P74. Request you identify our position, Farne skipper.'

The other Aldis went berserk.

'Motor vessel *My Joanna*. No obligation to assist your navigation. Will give you ten minutes from now figures 21.50 hours to accept my instructions and adopt course magnetic figures 07 degrees. If you do not comply we shall board you with naval party. Felice.'

I pressed the phone strip and called Genoa. Felice must have fixed them and they didn't acknowledge my call. I switched channels and called Nice who came up through a babble of static. I asked for a relay call to a London number. London was faint but free of static and I asked for the news editor and got his deputy.

'*Daily Mail* news desk. Who is that calling?'

'My name is Max Farne – F-A-R-N-E. I am skipper of a British registered vessel *My Joanna*. M-Y – J-O-A-N-N-A. I am in international waters twenty miles due south of Portofino and I am being attacked by a patrol boat of the Italian Navy.'

There were a few seconds of silence and then the voice came up with a surge of static.

'Did you say you were being attacked?'

'Yes.'

'Is this a hoax, Mr Farne? A PR stunt or something?'

'Absolutely not.'

'Have you contacted British authorities in Italy?'

'Not yet.'

'Why are you phoning us?'

'I want you to publicize this attack at once.'

'Have you phoned any other newspaper?'

'No.'

There were indistinct voices as I listened with the earpiece pressed tight against my ear.

'Are you there, Mr Farne? Can you hear me?'

'Yes.'

'We will check with our Rome man and with our

stringer in Milan. And maybe we can come back to you.'

'When will you do this?'

'We're on the phone to Rome at the moment. Goodbye.'

And then there was just static and a voice crackled through.

'Nice radio. Nice radio. Your call was seven minutes. Charges are three hundred *francs nouvelles*. OK?'

'OK.'

'*Bon soir.*'

And then we were back from dreamland to reality. I tried to sort out what to signal to Felice and couldn't make it. I flashed him on the Aldis and he came back quickly to acknowledge.

'Motor vessel *My Joanna* to patrol boat P74 Italian Navy. Have just telephoned London *Daily Mail* giving details of my position and your action. They are telephoning Rome as of now. If you attempt to board I shall open fire. Responsibility yours. Farne.'

A 'T', a single dash, came up and the light flickered and faded and then there was darkness.

I watched them carefully and minutes later they headed towards us, the searchlight sweeping the sea between. Even the sweeps of the light seemed angry, and as the patrol boat closed on us they were gathering speed – she swept alongside us about ten feet clear and then cut across our bows, and turned to come down the other side. Their weight sent walls of water smashing against our hull, but despite the noise we could take plenty of that. Then I saw what he was doing. They were taking a fast run across our stern and as they cut the rope of the starboard drogue we swung in a sickening lurch, and as the port drogue came away we swung back again. The audio signals and the little red lights were flashing and pinging as I scrabbled to cut out the auto-pilot.

Gabby was sitting on the foam seat with her legs braced against the table and I loved her right then because she was grinning as if it were all great fun.

Then our old friend P74 was charging down alongside us and great solid masses of water thudded down on the decks and fountained up the saloon windows. I guessed that they were getting just as uncomfortable a ride as we were. The difference now was that I knew he had decided that he didn't dare risk what would happen if he tried to board us. He'd opted for frightening us instead. Gabby relied on me, and I'd given up that sort of fright before Felice went to school.

Then the speaker crackled and Genoa were calling us. They had a call from London, was the skipper available to take it.

I clamped the rubber earpiece hard against my ear and through the surge and swell of static a voice was calling my name.

'Farne speaking. Who is that?'

'News editor *Daily Mail*. What is the situation now?'

'We are being harassed by the patrol boat. He is trying to carve us up. What news have you got?'

'What . . .?'

'What news at your end?'

'Italian Defence Ministry deny your allegations. British Embassy have no knowledge of you. What do you say?'

'They are both liars.'

'Why should they lie?'

'They are afraid of publicity.'

'About what?'

'About Italian Mafia smuggling hard drugs to United States.'

There was some heavy static, Genoa radio cut in and then went out again. Somebody wanted to hear the rest.

'Can you substantiate your story?'

'Yes, I can tell you where two million dollars' worth of heroin is hidden.'

'Is what?'

'Is hidden, for Christ's sake.'

'What do you want us to do?'

'Inform all other newspapers and the BBC and tell the Italian press as well.'

'Can you give a reference in Italy?'

'Yes.'

'Who is it?'

'They will arrest him or knock him off if I give his name. Why not come over.'

'Will you agree exclusive if we proceed?'

'When will you take action?'

'Immediately. We will share general details with P.A. Reuter and instruct their man in your area.'

'OK.'

'Will you accept one thousand pounds for exclusivity?'

'Agreed.'

'OK. Including photographs and interviews?'

'Yes.'

'OK. Best of British. Sleep well.'

Sleep well. I hung up and P74 was slicing across our bows as if we weren't there. Their angry wake breaking over our pulpit and sending the foredeck under a ton of water as it ran foaming down our sides.

I called up Nice radio and made it a Mayday call and they cleared the channel for me and I reported that I was being harassed by an Italian Navy patrol boat in international waters off the French coast. They took all the details eagerly. I knew that would stir them up and if it got around to extradition from France that wouldn't help the boys in Rome.

I broke open the brandy ration for both of us, and although I was exhausted I was a bit pleased with myself. I picked up the Aldis and staggered up the companionway to the afterdeck and set her flashing. Felice's boys were flashing back a couple of minutes later. I signalled that I wanted to talk boat-to-boat on channel 14. There was a long gap while he made the big decision but finally they flashed back a 'yes'.

As I went back down to the saloon I looked at my watch. It was midnight. I switched the VHF radio to channel 14 and called him up. He was on net in seconds.

'Felice here, officer commanding patrol boat number P74.'

'I want to put on record your reckless seamanship, Felice, and I want to inform you that I have notified the French authorities and a British national newspaper.'

There was a moment's silence. 'Informed them of what?'

'Of your deliberate harassment in international waters and of the Mafia heroin connection.'

'So what do I do – cry?'

'I suggest you inform your superiors, Felice. You're going to have a very bad press.'

It was clear enough to hear his vibrant anger.

'So maybe we have a day of national mourning. But you will be where you belong, *amico* – in jail.'

'Are you continuing your harassment, Captain?'

'Of course.'

'OK. I want to warn you that our conversation is being taped and probably monitored. Five minutes from now I am laying course south-west from here, 240 degrees magnetic. I shall put her on auto-pilot at seven knots. My crew and I will go up on the afterdeck where you can see us. The boat will stay on course. Nothing will deflect her unless you hit us. I shall notify Genoa and Nice to this effect so that if we sink, then the responsibility will be yours. Understood?'

He crashed down his phone and there was nothing but a distant voice calling up Livorno.

I went back and set the auto-pilot and laboured through a report to Nice and Genoa. Nice could barely conceal his excitement and Genoa sounded as though he thought that the bearers of bad news still got their heads chopped off.

Gabby had made up a flask of coffee and some biscuits and I took her hand and we went up on deck. The search-light swung straight to us and we stood there hand in hand as the white light made us squint. Gianni's daughter and me. With the glaring light still on us we sat in the fishing seats and when Gabby reached down to put the flask on the grating I lifted my arm to the bright light and gave Felice and his boys the 'V' sign. You get a bit childish when the pressure goes on too long.

The sea was calm and the patrol boat was at least fifty feet away on our port beam and they had doused the searchlight. The moonlight must have been bright enough for them to keep us under observation. As I munched a biscuit I decided it was time to get the views of what the politicians call the 'grass-roots'.

'You want to come back with me, sweetie?'

She looked up at me, the big blue eyes wide and troubled.

'Of course, Max. If you want, that is.'

'I think it would be best, Gabby. Things are going to be messy around Santa Margherita for a month or two.'

She laughed, and her head went back.

'You really are terrible, Max. You ought to have been a pirate.'

'Not me, lady – Felice is the pirate. But back to you. Are you sure you don't mind leaving Italy?'

She looked up, the blonde hair lifting in the gentle breeze.

'I don't really belong anywhere special, Max, it's no problem.'

And there wasn't a second of self-pity in her voice as she spoke. It was just a fact. But it made me swallow hard before I spoke.

'We'll have a nice long holiday when we get there, sweetie, cruising around Chichester, showing you the sights.'

And for ten minutes or so I gave her a picture of the cathedral and the Pallants and the creeks and the flea-pit cinema by the market hall, that always seemed to be showing a rerun of *Genevieve*. And I guess that there was probably some guy jilling around in Chichester creek telling his bird about what they'd do when they left it all behind and did the sights of Santa Margherita.

I put down the sleeping bag on the deck and we snuggled down. I wasn't bluffing with Felice; I meant to get some sleep but I had eased the butterfly nuts on the life-raft container. And despite all that Gabby softness I must have been asleep in seconds.

It was the Cessna that finally woke me. It was circling round us and a man with a long lens on his camera was poking it out of a window. They were about a hundred feet up and as I stood up the pilot waved and I waved back. Over our port bow the patrol boat looked white and innocent as she lay off at least a hundred feet. The sky was solid blue and I looked at my watch. It was ten o'clock. As I looked up again at the Cessna they waggled their wings, circled slowly and headed off due north.

Gabby was still sleeping so I trundled down to the wheel-house. I took the beacon fixes from La Spezia and Genoa and roughly plotted our position. I took the fixes again and used the dividers very carefully. They confirmed the first fix. Something must have pulled us slowly to starboard. We were about twelve miles south-east off Savona, about nine miles in a direct line from the nearest coast.

I brewed up some tea, made an omelette and went up to wake Gabby. As I stood up from speaking to her I looked across at the patrol boat and I could hardly believe my eyes. There was another Navy boat about a mile away and heading in our direction. They must really mean business to need two Navy boats to tackle a 40 footer armed with a pistol. They were probably going to give us the old nutcracker treatment as brought to perfection in the cod war off Iceland. The roughest you can get at sea without opening fire.

Back in the saloon we finished off the omelette and the tea, and while Gabby was having a shower I went to change channels on the VHF set. Like an idiot I had left the volume turned low and I had probably missed a lot of calls.

I tried Nice first and the operator sounded like a hotel manager trying to please a special guest.

'Yes, Monsieur Farne, two London numbers for you to call. We tried to raise you every half-hour but there was no response. We have heard Genoa calling you frequently. Maybe you contact them first, eh?'

A nod's as good as a wink, and I called Genoa on Channel 16. There was a touch of the funeral parlour about the Genoa operator. A mixture of formality, business and an underlying apprehension.

'Two calls for you *My Joanna*. Can you note the numbers – Genoa 61466 and Santa Margherita di Ligure 81326.'

I asked for the Genoa number first and seconds later they were on the line.

'Signor Farne?'

'Yes.'

'Ah, this is Ribaldi for P.A. Reuter and the *Daily Mail*. We have been trying to contact you. Did you see our photographer in the Cessna?'

'Yes, I saw him.'

189

'Good. I think we are making some progress for you. Have you spoken to Avvocato Mantoni yet?'

'No.'

'He is on his way out to you. Navy patrol boat P37. He has been retained by us to help you – we did some checking in Santa Margherita. He is acceptable to you, I hope.'

'Yes and no.'

'Will you keep in touch with us when you have spoken to him?'

'OK.'

'Can we speak to Signorina Podoni?'

'No.'

There was a pause.

'Is it true that she is the daughter of Gianni Podoni?'

'Yes.'

'Have you enough food and water?'

'Ample.'

'Sorry, I don't understand.'

'Yes, we have plenty.'

'And fuel?'

'We're OK.'

'*Ciao*, Signor Farne. We'll be in touch.'

I called for the Santa Margherita phone number but there was no response. It was probably Mantoni's.

Gabby was wearing one of my shirts and looked as fresh and bright as the morning. We went up together to the afterdeck to survey the scene.

The second patrol boat was alongside the P74 and we could only see her superstructure. She was older and bigger than our friend and there was a radar scanner on top of her wheelhouse. There were bodies moving about on deck but without my binoculars I couldn't make out who was who, and I didn't want to look that interested.

Gabby was swinging her legs and looking at me.

'What do you think's going to happen, Max?'

'I'm not sure, honey. I'm damn sure that the Italians will want to keep the heroin bit out of the news, even the Americans will want that. And they'll want to get at the stuff before the rest of the gang get to it.'

'Why did you contact the newspaper?'

'Mainly because there was no other choice – no other source of help. The Embassy and the Consulate would have been back long ago if they intended helping. They will know about the patrol boat and they're turning a blind eye. Now that P.A. Reuter and the *Mail* are in on the act the Embassy will have to bear down on the Italians. Before, they could say they didn't know what was going on. Now, they can't plead ignorance.'

'So what will happen?'

'They're sending out Avvocato Mantoni as a go-between.'

'What do you want to happen?'

'Number one, avoid going to jail. Number two, get back safe and sound with you to England. And lastly I don't want the boat to be sequestered by the Italians. That's about it.'

'Look, Max,' and she pointed. A ship's boat was coming over to us. I could make out three people but not who they were. Five minutes later it was alongside. There was Felice, Mantoni with a red leather brief-case, and a rating sitting in the stern.

I stood at the guard-rails looking down. Mantoni

avoided my glance, sitting there looking like Toad messing about in boats. Felice stood up, and looking at me, shouted, 'I am bringing Avvocato Mantoni on board. Those are my instructions, Farne.'

I lifted off the chain and slid down the bathing ladder and slammed home the hooks with the palm of my hand. Bent down, my face wasn't too far from Felice's. I waited until he put his arm out to grasp the ladder and I shouted down to him.

'Don't try it, Felice. Let Mantoni come alone and then you get back to your boat.'

He put one white-stockinged leg on to the bottom rung, his red face looking up at me.

'There are several witnesses, Felice. I warn you, if you come up the ladder you'll go in the drink.' And as his eyes glared at me he hesitated. He was near enough now for me not to need to shout.

'Try it, Felice. I'd enjoy putting my foot in your face.'

He knew I meant it. He wasn't a coward, just didn't want to give me any enjoyment. He held the ladder with his big hand to keep the boats together and he waved to Mantoni.

Mantoni was too big to be jumping around on boats but he came up the ladder with solemn dignity and turned and reached down as Felice held up the red brief-case.

Mantoni turned to face me and as he shook hands I thought I saw the flicker of a wink.

We all went down to the saloon, Mantoni taking up all one side of the bench, the red brief-case on the table.

'Now,' he said. 'We'd better start talking. What's going on?'

'What have you heard already?'

He sighed and leaned back on the seat. 'I have had a vivid scene-setting description by the police of two corpses found at the garage at Monza. I had already heard on the grape-vine about Franceschi's death. Two journalists have told me next to nothing about a valuable hoard of drugs of some kind whose where-abouts are known only to you – and I hear that you are making a bloody nuisance of yourself now, with one Guido Felice, captain in the Italian Navy. Is there *more*?' and the big eyes bulged out in mock concern.

'Have the Italians spoken to you at all?'

'What do you mean, the Italians? I'm an Italian, the police are Italians, the journalists are Italians. Who have you in mind – the Prime Minister?'

'Avvocato, I'm tired of being pressured. I want to get back to England. What do we do?'

'Ah,' he said. 'First the two bodies. Did you kill them?'

'On or off the record?'

'For now – off the record.'

'Yes. In self-defence.'

'Tell me the whole story.'

And I went through everything that mattered from the day I had arrived. Mantoni looked at Gabby and then back at me. He opened the brief-case, took out a pad and reached into his jacket pocket for a pen. He flipped open the cover of the pad, wrote something and then underlined it. He looked up at me again.

'Let's check what we've got to offer and what we want. Agreed?'

'Sure.'

'We can tell them where the heroin is?'

I nodded.

'We can make a statement regarding Lunghi and Monfalcone?' He looked at me, eyebrows raised.

'OK,' I said.

'And we could give an undertaking not to give details to the press, or radio, or TV, and the like.'

'We could.'

'And we want an undertaking that no charges are left on the record, no lien of any kind on the boat, free passage for boat and crew – that's about it.'

'Not quite.'

'What else?'

'I want all the repairs for the damage to the boat and its equipment paid for by them.'

He pursed his lips. 'What are we talking about? Fifty sterling, a hundred, or what?'

'Call it two hundred.'

He scribbled on his pad.

'How about if they ask you to pay for smashing up Monfalcone's Ferrari?'

'Who would ask? Has he got a widow? Nobody else is entitled to ask.'

Mantoni folded over the cover of his pad.

'You do realize that you're accused of serious crimes. You and Podoni seem to imagine that the rules aren't made for you. When the likes of you go boom-boom it's all OK because the victim is one of the bad guys. And *you* decide who's a bad guy.'

'No, I don't, Avvocato, neither did Gianni, so far as I know. But when men threaten my life and point guns at me and mine, I just shoot first. There ain't time to refer to some paragraph of the Coda Penale.'

He sniffed and gave me a long, hard look. He just wanted to make clear that I shouldn't think he was handling a nice easy case or that Avvocato Mantoni went along with my crude ethics. I didn't really care what Mantoni thought but I hadn't liked him pointing the finger at Gianni in front of Gabby.

He shuffled along the bench and stood up. He was almost at the bottom of the companionway when he turned round.

'Will you go along with whatever deal I do for you?'

I shook my head, but I managed a smile. ''Fraid not, Avvocato. You've written down the pluses and minuses. That's what I want, that's what I'll give in return.'

He nodded briskly as if he had had enough, turned to the step and hauled his way up to the deck. We stood there, the three of us, waiting for the boat to come over. This time the rating was alone and I helped Mantoni back down the steps. He didn't look back as the boat went off.

The auto-pilot signals were clicking every two or three minutes and it was obvious that something was making us yaw. I tried more revs and fewer revs but it made no difference. I adjusted the trim and fixed it so that we only pinged every five minutes.

I had been dodging one issue, and when we were drinking on deck I let it walk through my mind – young Gabby had no home, no background except her mother, and now that Lunghi was dead, no financial support. I decided that the money Lunghi had paid me for the boat had better be put in a fund for her. She was welcome to stay with me as long as she liked but I had to face the fact that I was a couple of years older than her dad. Maybe back in England and away from all the pressure I would think of some better solution.

It was mid-afternoon when the little boat came back again and Mantoni heaved himself up the ladder. He waved us imperiously to the saloon and Gabby poured him a drink as he subsided into place. He mopped his face with a white linen handkerchief and then dabbed at the back of his neck.

'I've worked out a deal, Farne. Hope you like it. In return for no charges being brought against you you will produce a sworn statement for the police about your experiences with Lunghi and Monfalcone.

'You will inform the Ministry of Justice where the heroin is and you will pay compensation of a token nature for scrapping the Ferrari.

'In return for this you will be shown every courtesy and allowed to proceed to wherever you want.'

'What about compensation for my boat damage?'

He shrugged. 'How about we offset that against the Ferrari?'

'OK.' I said it softly because I had a feeling that there was more to come. There was.

'Just one condition they make.'

I shook my head. 'No conditions. A deal is a deal.'

His big hand slapped the table. 'For God's sake man, listen before you speak. They might want you to be Mayor of Milan or something.'

'OK. I'm listening.'

He spoke quietly, not looking at me, busy with removing imaginary specks from his jacket.

'They want to save face all round. They want you to come back to Genoa. Make the statements for the police, et cetera, et cetera, and the story for the press will be that you have been assisting the police all the time. Great hero stuff.'

'We go into port without escort?'

'If that's what you want.'

'OK. It's a deal.'

The Aldis from P74 flickered out confirmation of the deal half an hour later and I signalled back that I should berth at Genoa about nine the next morning.

It was that odd time between afternoon and evening when the Mediterranean light turns the sky and the sea from blue to turquoise, and then pale green, and we stood on deck watching as the patrol boats turned and headed north-east. Suddenly, everywhere was quiet and still. The sea was smooth and heavy and the low sun dappled the swell and made lace patterns from the sudden riffles of the offshore breeze. After weeks of tension and days of physical pressure we were just like everybody else. A man and a girl on a boat. The time our own. It was like being let out of prison, and it had happened too quickly to be absorbed at once.

I've read somewhere that when great pressures are applied to human beings and then removed, that their minds turn automatically to procreation. That after the bombing of Guernica the survivors went out into the fields and made love. And there's no doubt that for the first time in two days I noticed that my white shirt looked remarkably different when worn by Gabby. When I looked up from the bulge of her breasts and their spiky tips to her face, she was smiling that amused girl-smile that says its owner knows exactly what you're thinking, and what you want to do, and is seconding the motion.

Gabby, still smiling, put out her hand and took mine and as we went down the companionway I was no longer in charge. I'd never made love to Gabby without some threat hanging over us and as I sat on the double bunk I watched her unbutton the shirt. When it slid down her arms she was naked and she stood there smiling as I looked at her. The clear blue eyes, the neat upturned nose and the gorgeous orange-coloured mouth were framed by the long blonde hair that went down to her shoulders to flow on to the tops of her breasts. She must have been watching my eyes because her hands pushed the hair behind her shoulders so that I could see all of the big mounds and the pale pink circles at their tips. There was a bruise on the flat young belly and another on her hip where it flowed down to the blonde bush between her long, shapely legs.

I was conscious of the full, firm mounds trembling as she walked over to the bunk, and then she was astride me, the blonde hair like a waterfall around my face. My hands opened wide to take the weight of the smooth, resilient breasts and her body clamped eagerly to mine.

It was midnight when I was sipping tea and looking over the charts. We had done another three hours in the wrong direction and I set the auto-pilot on the north-east course and put the revs up on both engines so that we were doing 10–11 knots.

We both slept for two hours and I took over from the autopilot and slid both levers up to give us 15 knots.

Genoa has a million inhabitants and Wagner once said it was 'indescribably beautiful'. However, that description does not apply to the port itself. But as we thumped our way into the Bacino delle Grazie there was a touch of magic as the sun turned the yellow bricks to gold, and as we rounded the mole the harbour-master radioed and directed us to the Ponte Spinola.

I turned her round and went in astern and two men in blue jerseys took our lines and made fast for us.

There was quite a reception committee. Mantoni and two others, and another one with a camera. Two police officers in uniform. Felice and two other naval officers, and half-a-dozen assorted bodies. When the engines were silent I slid back the saloon door and waved to Mantoni.

His two mates were from the Ministry of Justice and they spent an hour taking statements from me and from Gabby, and official seals were pressed to red sealing wax.

The police came, next. All amiability and co-operation, and we fixed for them to come back after lunch.

The man from the *Daily Mail* and his mate from Reuters took one look at Gabby and waved frantically to the photographer.

Messages were sent to buy bikinis, tight sweaters and minuscule briefs. Meantime we told them the tale.

They were there for three hours and they wanted more time the next day when they had spoken to the Ministry of Justice and the police. They didn't bat an eye when I told them that I was mistaken about the harassment, and it looked as if it was all going to be Felice and Gabby.

For three days we made statements, added subsidiary statements, agreed story angles, were photographed, were lunched on board the P74, bought clothes for Gabby and stores for the boat and then it was all over. Mantoni and Felice waved to us from the quayside as we chugged our way out on the Sunday evening.

We kept a sort of fretwork course around the southern coast of Spain, up the Portuguese coast and finally spent our last foreign night at Honfleur.

At four o'clock the following afternoon we came over the Chichester bar at full flood. We locked through to Birdham Pool half an hour later.

There was one last postscript to that summer. Two weeks after we got back I reckoned it was time to start checking over the boat. We stayed at The Ship in Chichester for a couple of days while she was slipped at the boatyard and they scraped and cleaned the hull. There was enough growth on her to have caused the trouble with the auto-pilot.

When we were back on the boat I started on her from the chain locker backwards so it was another three weeks before I got the gratings up on the after deck. I ran the bilge pump and cleaned out the sludge and the water, and mopped the last refuse out. There are two banks of batteries, four a side, and I unscrewed the connections and toted each battery up to the quayside for the yard to pick up and charge.

Where the batteries had been was a solid mass of grease between the battery mountings, and I collected a pile of old rags to clear it away. How it had got there was beyond my understanding. There was nothing there that needed to be greased.

The grease looked about four inches thick and I jammed in a screwdriver to test its solidity. I thought I'd broken my wrist as the screwdriver hit solid metal. I used some rag to move the layer of grease, and there were solid blocks of metal about the size of house bricks. Even in the filth I knew what they were. They were why Lunghi had taken the boat for two days. They were Lunghi's insurance against disaster. They were why he paid the high price for the boat. And they were why the steering had gone to hell on the auto-pilot. They were blocks of gold, about nine inches by four by two. I prised one up with the screwdriver and it was heavy in my hand, at least ten pounds.

When I got them all up there were thirty of them and I wrapped them in three old towels and shoved them into one of the seat lockers along with nylon ropes and plastic fenders.

It took four weeks to get rid of the gold and they raised 210,000 dollars US. The Mr Patel who bought them has a grocer's shop in one of the side streets off Chiswick High Street, and I'd guess he would make another 50,000 on the top.

Right now Gabby is sitting on that locker in a pale blue bikini, her eyes on the tip of a red float that's meant to signal the arrival of a hungry roach. Her mother's coming down for the day tomorrow and I've put the dollars in a Bahamas bank account for her. I've got a feeling it's going to be one of the best winters I've ever had.